DRACULA

'Welcome to my house. Enter of your own free will.' As soon as I went through the doorway, he rushed forward. He grabbed my hand. The power of his grip made me gasp with pain. His hand felt as cold as ice. It was more like the hand of a dead man than a living man.

'Count Dracula?' I asked.

He bowed. 'Yes. I am Dracula,' he replied. 'You are welcome to my house, Mr Harker. Come in. The night air is cold, and you need to eat and rest.'

Dracula

Bram Stoker
Adapted by Jim Alderson

SPARROW
BOOKS

A Sparrow Book
Published by Arrow Books Limited
17-21 Conway Street, London W1P 6JD

An imprint of the Hutchinson Publishing Group

London Melbourne Sydney Auckland
Johannesburg and agencies
throughout the world

This adaptation first published by Hutchinson in
their Bulls-Eye series 1978
Sparrow edition 1983
Reprinted 1983

Printed and bound in Great Britain by
Anchor Brendon Ltd, Tiptree, Essex

ISBN 0 09 930350 7

Contents

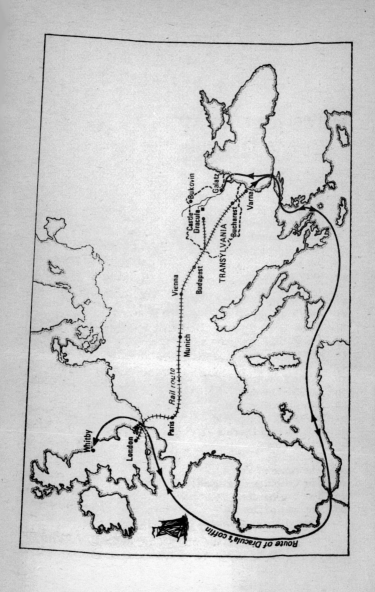

Route of Dracula's coffin

Whitby
London
Paris
Rail route
Munich
Vienna
Budapest
TRANSYLVANIA
Castle Dracula
Bukovin
Galatz
Bucharest
Varna

1 The journey to Castle Dracula

Jonathan Harker's diary

My name is Jonathan Harker. I work for a lawyer called Mr Hawkins. Mr Hawkins has sent me to meet a man called Count Dracula. This Count lives in an old castle in Transylvania. I do not know him at all. Mr Hawkins wants me to help this Count to buy a large old house in England. I will meet him in two days' time. I wonder what he will be like?

2 May – After travelling all day, I stopped for the night at a hotel in Budapest. I kept thinking of Castle Dracula. For some odd reason I had all sorts of strange dreams. Perhaps it was the wine I had drunk or perhaps it was the dog that kept howling all night under my window.

3 May – This morning I went on by train. We went through some of the most beautiful countryside I have ever seen. After a while, we arrived at a small town in Transylvania. Count Dracula had ordered me to go to a hotel in the town so I went there at once. I was met by an old peasant woman in a white apron. When I came close she bowed and said, 'Are you the Englishman?'

'Yes,' I said, 'I am Jonathan Harker.'

She smiled. Then she gave some messages to an old man in a white shirt. He went away but came back at once. He had a letter. It was from the Count:

My friend – Welcome to my country. I am looking forward to seeing you. Sleep well tonight. At three tomorrow you will get on the stage-coach for Bukovin. At the Borgo Pass my own carriage will meet you. Then it will bring you to me. I trust that your journey from London has been a happy one, and I hope you will enjoy yourself in my beautiful land.

Your friend,
Dracula

4 May – I asked the landlord if he knew Count Dracula. I wanted to know if he could tell me anything of the Count's castle. The old man and his wife looked at one another. They look frightened. They made the sign of the cross. They said they knew nothing and would not say another word on the matter. It was very nearly time to catch the stage-coach. I had no chance to ask anyone else about the mysterious Count. I did not know why they were afraid. I was beginning to feel worried.

Just before I left, the old lady came to my room. She was trembling with terror.

'Do you have to go?' she said. 'Do you really have to?' She was so excited I could not understand what she was saying. I told her I had to go at once. I had important things to do.

'Do you know what day it is?' she asked. I said that it was the fourth of May. She shook her head:

'It is the night before St George's Day,' she said. 'On this night, as the clock strikes twelve, all the evil things in the world can have power over you. Do you know where you are going? Do you know what it is you are going to?'

She was very upset indeed. I tried to comfort her but with no success. Then she went down on her knees. She begged me not to go. She asked me to wait at least a day or two before starting. I thought she was mad. I told her I simply had to visit the Count on business and nothing must stop me. She got up and dried her eyes. Then she gave me a cross to put round my neck. How strange! Still, to keep her quiet I did what she wanted. I put the cross around my neck.

I am beginning to feel rather frightened. I wish I was at home with Mina, the woman I am going to marry.

The coach came at last. The driver got down and started talking to the old lady. A crowd gathered round. Everyone kept looking at me with pity. I kept hearing the words 'Satan', 'hell', 'witch' and 'vampire'. I just did not understand what all the fuss was about.

As we started, the crowd crossed themselves. I asked a fellow passenger why they did this. He told me that it was a defence against demons and evil. I shall never forget that crowd of people. They were all crossing themselves. The coach driver cracked his big whip over his four small horses. We set off on our journey.

The scenery was so beautiful I soon forgot about my fears. We passed forests, woods full of flowers and orchards full of fruit. The afternoon sun shone on the mountains. But after a time the shadows began to creep around us. It began to get very cold. The roads were getting steeper and the horses were growing tired. When it was dark, the passengers became worried. They shouted at the driver. The driver lashed at his horses until they bled. Suddenly the coach stopped. There were dark clouds overhead. I could feel the thunder in the air. I looked for the carriage which would take me to the Count. The driver waited for a while. Then he called to me in German:

'You are lucky. You are not expected after all. We will go on to the next town.' But as he spoke the horses began to snort. They kicked so wildly that the driver had to hold the reins tight. The passengers screamed and crossed themselves. A carriage pulled by four coal-black horses came along the road towards us. A tall man with a long brown beard was driving. His eyes were very bright. In the lamplight they seemed to be a bright red.

He said to our driver, 'You are early tonight, my friend.'

The driver was terrified.

'The Englishman was in a hurry,' he said.

'Is that why you wanted to take him to the next town?' asked the stranger. 'You cannot trick me, my friend. I know too much and my horses are too fast for you.' As he spoke, he smiled. The lamplight fell on a hard-looking mouth. He had very red lips and sharp-looking teeth. They were as white as ivory. Our driver crossed himself. Soon I was inside the carriage. I watched the coach. It disappeared into the darkness.

My new driver gave me a bottle of plum brandy to keep me warm. Then we set off. I struck a match and looked at my watch. It was almost midnight. This gave me a shock. I remembered the words of the old lady. I felt almost sick with fear.

A dog howled as if it was afraid. Other dogs howled in the distance. The horses began to rear. The driver spoke to them and they settled down again. From the window I could see they were shivering and sweating. Then I heard a louder and sharper howling. It was wolves! The carriage suddenly turned down a narrow road to the right.

There were trees all round us. The wind whistled through them and their branches crashed together as we swept along. It grew colder and colder. Snow began to fall. It covered everything with a white blanket. We could still hear the howling of dogs, which then grew fainter. But the baying of the wolves sounded nearer and nearer. It was as though they were closing round us from every side. I became very frightened and so did the horses. But the driver was not in the least worried.

The carriage stopped. The moon suddenly appeared from behind some black clouds. I saw a ring of wolves. They were all round us. They had white teeth and huge red tongues. Their bodies were long and thin, and their hair was shaggy. They were not howling. They watched us in complete silence. I was frozen stiff with fear. The horses jumped about in terror. I yelled to the driver. I told him to try and burst through this ring of death before we were torn to pieces. The driver stood up and threw both arms in the air. To my amazement the wolves stepped back. They howled softly and disappeared into the darkness. This was so strange I began to shiver. I was not able to speak or move. A minute or two later, the driver pulled up the horses in the yard of a big ruined castle. No light came from the tall black windows, and the broken towers made a jagged line against the moonlit sky. So this was Castle Dracula!

2 Inside the castle

Jonathan Harker's diary (continued)

5 May – Midnight had passed when I got out of the coach. I waited outside a huge old door, studded with large iron nails. The driver placed my luggage beside me. Then he jumped back into his seat and drove off into the darkness.

I stood in silence. I did not know what to do. There was no sign of a bell or knocker. I knew my voice would not be heard through the dark windows and the thick stone walls. I waited for what seemed an endless time. I was beginning to feel very frightened. What sort of place had I come to? What sort of people would I meet? What terrible things were going to happen to me?

I had come to this place as a lawyer. All I wanted was to tell Count Dracula how to buy a place in London. I began to rub my eyes. I pinched myself to see if I was awake. It all seemed like a horrible nightmare to me. I expected to awake suddenly and find myself at home in London. But my arm hurt when I pinched it. This was no dream.

I heard a heavy step behind the great door. I looked through a chink and saw a light coming towards me. There was the sound of rattling chains. I heard the clanking of huge bolts being drawn back. A key turned with a loud scraping noise. The great door swung back.

A tall old man stood there. He was clean-shaven except for a long white moustache. He was dressed in black from head to foot and held an old silver lamp. This lamp sent long shadows over the door. The old man spoke very good English but his voice sounded rather odd.

'Welcome to my house. Enter of your own free will.'

As soon as I went through the doorway, he rushed forward. He grabbed my hand. The power of his grip made me gasp with pain. His hand felt as cold as ice. It was more like the hand of a dead man than a living man.

'Count Dracula?' I asked.

He bowed. 'Yes. I am Dracula,' he replied. 'You are welcome to my house, Mr Harker. Come in. The night air is cold, and you need to eat and rest.'

He picked up my bags and led me to a room. It was well lit. A table was laid for supper and some logs burned brightly in the fire. Then he showed me my bedroom. I had a wash and went down for supper.

'Please sit down and eat,' he said. 'I have already eaten and I do not drink.'

I handed him a letter from Mr Hawkins, the head of my firm. The Count read the letter. I told him all that had happened on the journey. As I talked, I looked at him more closely. He was an odd man. His face was strong and his eyebrows were very bushy. Under his white moustache, his mouth was cruel. His teeth were very pointed and stuck out over his red lips. His ears were white and pointed at the top. His skin was very, very pale. It was almost bloodless. His hands were thick and powerful. The nails were long and cut to sharp points. And there were hairs growing from the middle of his palms!

The Count leaned over to talk to me. I shivered. His breath was so bad I wanted to be sick all over the carpet. He noticed my shiver. He leaned back with a strange smile. For a while we were both silent. Then, I heard the wolves again. They were in the valley below.

The Count's eyes lit up and he said, 'Listen to them. They are the children of the night. What music they make!'

Then he got up and said, 'But you must be tired. Your bedroom is all ready. You may sleep as long as you wish. I will be away until tomorrow afternoon. Sleep well and have pleasant dreams!'

I went to my bedroom and sat down. For some reason or other I am terribly afraid. May God protect me!

I slept until the afternoon. When I woke, I found a cold breakfast laid out in the dining room. There was a note which said, 'I have to be away for a while. Do not wait for me. – D.'

I had a good meal and then explored the castle. To my amazement, I could not find a single servant. The rooms were full of beautiful paintings and furniture, but I could not find a mirror anywhere. I had to use a little mirror I had brought with me. The castle itself was silent – apart from the howling of wolves.

In the end, I found a library. I began reading some English books and magazines. The day passed very quickly. During the evening the Count came back. He said he was sorry for being late. We talked about London for a while. He told me I could go wherever I wanted in the castle – except where the doors were locked. I thanked him for his kindness and trust.

I then asked him to sign some papers. I told him

about the place he was buying in London. It was a large old house surrounded by gardens and ponds. Another building near the estate had been turned into a private lunatic asylum.

When I had finished, he said, 'I am glad that the house is old and big. It would kill me to live in a new house. I do not like noise and music. I prefer darkness and shadows. You see, I am no longer young.' I saw that the Count was smiling strangely when he said this, and I wondered why.

We talked until the early hours of the morning. Then all at once a cock crowed. Dracula leaped to his feet. He said he was sorry for keeping me up so late. Then he left me. I went to my bedroom. I watched the sky turn grey with the morning.

6 May – I am beginning to get very worried. The place is so strange. I never speak to anybody except the Count and I see him only in the evening. I wish I had never come to this place. I am afraid I may go mad.

I could not sleep much last night, so early in the morning I decided to shave. I hung my mirror by the bedroom window. I was just about to begin when I felt a hand on my shoulder. I heard the Count's voice saying to me, 'Good morning.' I jumped in alarm. I had not seen him in the mirror. I cut myself slightly in my surprise but did not notice this at once. After saying 'Good morning' to the Count I turned to look in the mirror again. I was amazed. The man was right behind me but I could not see him in the mirror! I then noticed the cut on my chin and turned to get some sticking plaster. When the Count saw my face, his eyes blazed like those of an angry demon. He made a grab for my throat. I stepped back and his hand fell upon the chain round my neck which held the cross. This made him stop at once. His terrible excitement passed so quickly I could hardly believe it.

'Take care,' he said, 'take care when you cut yourself. It is more dangerous than you think in this country.' Then he grabbed hold of the mirror.

'And this,' he said, 'is the thing that caused the trouble. It is a silly plaything for vain people. Away with it!' He opened the window with one pull of his terrible hand and flung the mirror out. It smashed into a thousand pieces on the yard below. Then he left without saying another word.

Later in the morning, I had breakfast alone. I could not find the Count anywhere. It is strange but I have not yet seen the Count eat or drink!

I then explored the castle again. I found that it stands on the edge of a very steep cliff. A stone falling from the window would drop a thousand feet without touching anything. All the doors are locked and bolted. I now know that this castle is a prison and I am a prisoner!

3 The first of the vampires

Jonathan Harker's diary (continued)

11 May, late evening, after dark – When I found that I was a prisoner, a wild feeling of panic came over me. I rushed up and down the stairs. I tried every door and looked through every window. In fact, I behaved like a rat in a trap. After a while, however, I sat down and tried to think. I knew that I must not let the Count know of my fear. I should need all my brains to get myself out of this trap.

While I was thinking, I heard the great door shut. The Count had returned. I spied on him. I saw him make his bed and lay the table in the dining room. It was then that I knew there were no servants. The driver with the strange power over the wolves must have been the Count in disguise! Why had those peasants crossed themselves? Why had that woman given me the cross? I decided to try to get Dracula to talk about himself. But I did not want him to suspect anything.

Midnight – I have had a long talk with the Count. I asked him a few questions about the history of his country. He seemed to know a lot about it. He described many battles and spoke like a king. I learned how, many years ago, the Draculas had defeated the Turks and made their blood flow like water.

Once again, as soon as the cock crowed, he left the room. Everything seems to stop at daybreak!

12 May – Last evening, the Count told me to write to Mr Hawkins. I was to tell him I would not be back for another month. He let me write a letter to Mina, the girl I am to marry. But I cannot tell her my real fears because I know he reads my mail.

As the Count was leaving, he stopped and said to me, 'Let me give you some advice, my dear young friend – or rather, let me warn you. If you leave this dining room or your bedroom, you must not go to sleep in any other part of the castle. It is an old castle with many memories. There are nightmares for those who sleep in some of the rooms. Be warned! If you feel sleepy, you must return to your own room. If you don't –' He finished by making a strange chopping movement with his hands. I shuddered. I knew what he meant.

Later – I hung a cross above my bed and left my room. I went up some stairs. I stood staring through a window at the south side of the castle. I took a deep breath of the night air and sighed. The valley looked so beautiful and I felt so unhappy. I leaned out of the window. Then I noticed something moving down below. The Count's head suddenly appeared from a window. At first I found it funny and wanted to call out. Then suddenly my feelings changed to horror. He climbed through the window. He began to crawl *face down* over the wall. He spread his cloak out like great wings. At first I could not believe my eyes. I thought it was some trick of the moonlight. But I kept looking and knew it was real. The Count was moving down the wall like a lizard.

What sort of man is this? Or what sort of creature is it? There is no escape for me. I dare not let my mind think too much . . . .

15 May – Once more I have seen the Count go moving like a lizard.

I decided to explore the castle further. After a time, I managed to force a lock. I found myself in a room which must have been used hundreds of years ago by the ladies of the castle. I like this room. It is much more attractive than my own bedroom. I will stay here. The place has a feeling of peace.

16 May – God keep me sane! Or perhaps I am already mad. This place is full of evil, hateful things!

After last writing in my diary, I began to feel sleepy. I remembered the Count's warning but decided to disobey him. I knew he was a liar about other things. I decided to sleep in the room where ladies had lived in the old days. I lay down on a couch. I fell asleep only to wake again to a living nightmare!

I was not alone in the room. In the moonlight opposite me were three young women. They wore long white dresses but made no shadow on the floor. They came close to me. They looked at me and whispered together. Two were dark with large eyes that seemed almost red in the pale moonlight. The other had long golden hair. All three had brilliant white teeth. Their teeth shone like pearls against the ruby redness of their soft lips. I was frightened but curious. I very much wanted them to kiss me with those red lips. I hope Mina never reads this, but it is true. They whispered together. Then all three laughed. It was a musical laugh, but a strange and terrible sound. The fair girl shook her head as if to tease me. The other two told her to go on.

One said, 'Go on! You are the first. We will follow.'

The other said, 'He is strong. There are enough kisses for us all.'

I lay quietly and looked from under my eyelashes. I wanted her to kiss me. I was dying for her to kiss me. The fair girl bent over me. I could feel her breath. It was as sweet as honey but it also had the horrible smell of dried blood.

The girl went on her knees and bent over me. She licked her lips like an animal. In the moonlight I could see that her lips were wet. Her red tongue licked her sharp white teeth. Lower and lower went her head. The lips went below the level of my mouth and chin.

They seemed about to stop on my throat. Then she waited. I could hear the horrible clicking sound of her tongue. It licked her teeth and lips and I could feel her hot breath on my neck. The skin on my throat began to tingle. I could feel the soft, shivering touch of her lips on the skin of my throat. I could feel the hard tips of two sharp teeth, just touching. I closed my eyes and waited. I waited with a beating heart.

But at that moment something else moved in front of me. It was the Count. He was very angry. My eyes opened. I saw him grab the girl by the neck. He dragged her back. Her blue eyes were filled with hate and her teeth made a crunching sound. But the Count! He was like a demon from hell. His eyes were red and burned like flames. He hurled the woman back and raised his arms as he had done to drive off the wolves.

'How dare you touch him, any of you!' he shouted. 'Back, I tell you. This man belongs to me!'

'Are we to have anything tonight?' asked one of them. She gave a low laugh. She pointed to a bag which he had thrown on the floor. The bag moved. There was something alive in it. The Count nodded and one of the women sprang forward. I heard the gasp and low cry of a tiny child. The women laughed. I lay there helpless with horror. As if by magic, they became almost invisible. They seemed to float through the window. For a moment I saw their dim shapes outside. Then they vanished into the moonlight.

Suddenly I was overcome with horror and fainted.

4 No escape

Jonathan Harker's diary (continued)

I awoke in my own bed. Had I been dreaming or had the Count carried me here? I was glad of one thing. If the Count had carried me here and undressed me, he must have done it in a hurry because my pockets had not been searched. If he had found my diary, I know he would have destroyed it. I will never sleep in another room again. I hate my bedroom but nothing could be worse than those cruel women who are waiting to suck my blood!

18 May – I have been down to look at that room again in daylight. I wanted to find out if I had been dreaming. When I got to the door at the top of the stairs, I found it closed. It was locked from the inside. I know now it was no dream.

19 May – I know I am soon to die. Last night the Count told me to write a letter. The letter was to say that I had left the castle safely and had arrived at a nearby town. I knew I was his prisoner, so I had to agree. The Count said that the post was bad. He said that the letter would stop my friends from worrying. He told me to put the date of 29 June on the letter.

Now I know how long I have to live. He will kill me after 29 June. God help me!

28 May – There is a chance I might escape or at least send word home. A band of gypsies have set up camp in the yard below. I know they are brave people so I will write some letters. . . .

I have now written one letter to Mr Hawkins and another to Mina. I did not say too much in case the letters fall into the hands of the Count. . . .

Now, I have given the letters to the gypsies. I threw them through the bars of my window with a gold piece. I made signs that I wanted to have them posted. The man who took them bowed and put them in his cap. I could do no more, so I went back to my study and began to read. . . .

Later, the Count came up. He sat down beside me and handed me my two letters.

'The gypsies have given me these,' he said. He burned them up in front of me in the flame of a lamp. Then he went out of the room and I could hear the key turn softly. A minute later, I tried the door. It was locked.

31 May – When I woke today, I looked for my envelopes and writing paper. But they have gone. The Count has taken my suit, my overcoat and my rug as well.

17 June – The gypsies have gone. I am all alone.

24 June – Last night I saw the Count leave the castle. I decided to watch for his return. I sat for ages by the window. Then I began to notice some pretty little specks. They were floating in the rays of the moon. They were like tiny grains of dust and they seemed to be dancing. I watched them until I began to feel calm and sleepy.

Suddenly something made me sit up. I could hear the howling of dogs. The noise came from the valley which was hidden from my sight. It became louder and louder. The floating specks of dust turned into new shapes as they danced in the moonlight. I felt myself struggling to stay awake. I was becoming hypnotized. The dust danced more and more quickly. Suddenly I knew what it was. I ran screaming to my room. It was the three ghostly women!

A couple of hours later, I heard something stir in the Count's room. A sudden cry was followed by a deep and awful silence. I shuddered and wept.

I sat weeping on my bed. Then I heard a sound in the yard below. It was the terrible cry of a woman. I rushed to the window and looked out between the bars. It was indeed a woman. Her hair had fallen over her face. She was holding her hands over her heart, and she was out of breath from running. She was leaning against the corner of a gateway.

When she saw my face at the window she threw herself forward and yelled, 'Monster, give me my child!'

Above me, I heard the voice of the Count. He was calling in a strange voice. His call seemed to be answered by the howling of wolves. In a few moments a pack of them came running into the yard, and went for the woman.

Her cries soon stopped, and the wolves stopped howling. Then they ran away licking their lips.

I could not pity her. I knew what had become of her child. I knew she was better off dead.

What shall I do? What can I do? How can I escape from this dreadful place?

25 June, morning – I have only a few days left to live. I must do something!

It has always been at night when I have been in worst danger. I have not seen the Count in the day-light. Can it be that he sleeps when others are awake?

If I could only get into his room! But there is no possible way. The door is always locked.

Yes, there is one way, if I dare to take it! I will climb down the wall! I have seen him crawl out of his window. Why shouldn't I copy him and go in by his window? I do not stand much of a chance but I must risk it. The worst that can happen is that I fall and die. God help me in my task. Good-bye, Mina, if I fail!

Same day, later – I have made the effort and, God helping me, have come safely back to this room. I must put down every detail in order. I went to the window, took off my boots and climbed on a narrow ledge of stone. I looked down once. This made me dizzy and I almost fell. After that, I did not look down again. By some miracle I found the Count's room and slid feet-first through the window. I looked around for the Count but saw that the room was empty.

The floors were covered with dust. In one corner of the room was a heavy door, which was open. It led down a steep winding stairway. At the bottom was a dark tunnel. This tunnel had a sick, sour smell. The further I went, the worse the smell became. I pulled open a heavy door and found myself in an old, ruined chapel. This place must have once been used as a graveyard. There were steps leading down into what looked like an underground prison made up of three cells. In two of these cells I found nothing but bits of coffin and piles of dust. But in the third I found something else.

The third cell was filled with earth. But on top of the earth was a coffin, and inside lay the Count. He was either dead or asleep. His eyes were open but they looked like stone. His cheeks were warm and yet they were white as death. His lips were as red as ever but he had no pulse. There was no sign of life in him. I ran from the room, crawled up the castle wall again, threw myself panting upon my bed and tried to think.

29 June – By today, my letter will be on its way. I saw the Count leave the castle to post my letter, and he was wearing my clothes, so that the people in the village would think it was me.

The Count then came into my room this morning to tell me I am leaving tomorrow. I did not trust him.

'Why can't I go tonight?'

'Because my coachman and horses have gone away to get something for me.'

'But I don't mind walking. I want to get away at once.' The Count gave a cunning smile.

'Come with me, my dear young friend,' he said. 'I do not want to keep you here against your will. Come!' He led me down the stairs along the hall. Suddenly he stopped.

'Listen!'

The howling of wolves sounded very close. It was almost as if the sound started as he lifted up his hand. It was as if he had given the signal for the howling to begin. He unhooked the heavy chains and began to pull open the door.

The door began to open. The wolves howled louder and louder. I could see their red jaws and champing teeth. I could see their claws as they leapt at the opening door. I wondered if this was how I would die. I was afraid.

'Shut that door!' I yelled. 'I shall wait till morning!' We went back to the library in silence. I left the Count and went back to my bedroom. I lay down. Then I heard whispering at my door. I went to it softly and listened. I heard the voice of the Count.

'Get back to your own place! It is not your turn yet. Wait! Have patience! Tonight is mine. Tomorrow night is yours!' There was a low, sweet sound of laughter. In a rage I opened the door, to find the three terrible women. They were licking their lips. As I appeared they gave a horrible laugh, and ran away.

I came back to my room and threw myself on my knees. Is the end so near? Tomorrow! Tomorrow! Lord, help me!

30 June, morning – These may be the last words I ever write in this diary. I carry it with me always, and it is now the only thing I have left in the world.

I slept until dawn this morning. Then I crawled down the wall into the Count's room. It was empty. I went down the winding stair and along the dark passage till I came to the empty chapel. I knew now where to find the monster I was looking for. I pulled back the coffin lid and put it against the wall. And then I saw something which filled my soul with horror. There lay the Count but he looked very much younger. The white hair and moustache had changed to a dark grey. The cheeks were fatter and the white skin seemed ruby red underneath. The mouth was redder than ever. On the lips were tiny pools of fresh blood. The blood trickled from the corners of his mouth and ran over his chin and neck. It seemed as if this disgusting creature was filled up with other people's blood.

I searched him for the keys so that I could escape from this horrible place. But I could not find them. I stopped and looked at the Count. This was the creature I was helping to come to London. In that city he would drink the blood of helpless victims. He would make an army of demons just like himself. The very thought made me feel mad. I wanted to rid the world of such a monster. I grabbed a shovel and struck at his face. But as I did so, the head turned and I seemed to freeze. The shovel twisted in my hand. It struck the Count a blow on the forehead and bounced back against the side of the coffin. This made the lid fall and the Count's face was covered up again.

I sat down and tried to think. My brain was on fire. I could not think clearly. As I waited, I heard the sound of singing. It was the gypsies and they were coming nearer. I hid behind the door in the passage leading back to the Count's room. I was ready to make a dash for freedom if the gypsies opened the other door leading to the outside world. Suddenly a huge gust of wind caught the door behind which I was hiding. It slammed shut. I beat on it with my fists. But I could not move it. I was trapped. I heard the outside door open. Then I heard the sound of the coffin being taken away by singing gypsies. I yelled but no one answered.

I am alone with those terrible women. I must try to climb the wall again. It would be better to be smashed at the foot of the castle than become a victim to those creatures. Good-bye, Mina!

5 Mina waits in Whitby

Mina's diary

(*Note: Mina Murray is the woman Jonathan Harker wants to marry. She is in love with Jonathan. She does not know he is the prisoner of Dracula.*)

16 July – I have not had a letter from Jonathan for a long time. I wish he would get home soon. I am longing to hear all his news. It must be nice to see strange countries. I hope we will be able to see them when we are together.

I must write to my best friend Lucy. She tells me she is in love, but I do not know who the man is yet. There are a lot of men in her life. She is such a pretty girl! Here is what she said in her last letter to me:

My dearest Mina,   24 May
It never rains but it pours. I am only twenty years old but today I have had three proposals of marriage. Just fancy! THREE proposals in one day! Isn't it awful! I feel very sorry for two of the poor fellows. I will tell you everything but you simply must keep it a secret from *everyone*. Except your Jonathan, of course. The first proposal was from An American. He is Quincey P. Morris. I had to tell him I was in love with someone else. He was so disappointed, but he took it well. He smiled and said we would always be friends. What a pity we are not allowed to have two or three husbands!

The second proposal came from a man called Dr Jack Seward. He runs a lunatic asylum. The asylum is next to the place that Count Dracula wants to buy. Dr Seward is a man with a strong jaw. He has a good forehead and clear blue eyes. He was very nervous. I felt so sorry for him I burst into tears. When I told him I loved someone else, he said he was sorry. He wished me every happiness. Then he promised to be one of my best friends. You must excuse this letter being all blotchy but I have been crying.

Ever your loving,
Lucy

PS Oh, the third proposal. It was made by Arthur Holmwood. He is the man I have loved since I was a child. It was all very muddled. It seemed only a moment from his coming into the room till both his arms were around me and he was kissing me. I am very, very happy, and I don't know what I have done to deserve it. Good-bye.

PPS Do come and see me. I'll expect you on 24 July.

24 July, Whitby – Lucy met me at the station. She took me to her large house which overlooks the sea. I am very happy for Lucy and Arthur but I cannot help worrying about Jonathan. I wonder if he is still thinking about me. I wish he were here.

1 August – Still no news of Jonathan. This is really worrying. I am beginning to think something terrible may have happened to him.

Yesterday I met Dr Seward, one of the men who proposed to Lucy. He is a charming man, but I can't help shuddering when he talks about his patients. One of them has the habit of eating spiders and flies!!

I keep remembering that his lunatic asylum is almost next door to the new place of that Count. This makes me think of Jonathan. I miss him so much.

6 August – Still no news. I am very worried. No one has heard a word of Jonathan since May. I must pray to God for patience. Lucy is getting very nervous. Her marriage is near, and she has been walking in her sleep. I hope her health remains good for she is a very highly strung girl.

I went for a walk to the sea shore. A storm was blowing. The sailors were very worried. They could see a ship that was being battered by the storm wind. One old man said he could smell death in the air. Everybody was afraid. Oh Jonathan! I wonder if you too are dead.

6 Dracula's journey to Whitby

(*While Mina was waiting for news of Jonathan, Dracula was making his way to England. He had his coffin put on board a ship. But the ship was wrecked in a storm off Whitby.*

There was a report of the shipwreck in the Whitby newspaper. The reporter did not know that Count Dracula was on board the ship. Neither did he know that the Count could turn himself into a dog.)

From the *Daily News*, 7 August

SHIP CAUGHT IN STORM OFF WHITBY

Yesterday, a sudden storm hit the coast of Whitby. High seas swept people off their feet. There was a heavy fog, broken up by lightning. A foreign ship, caught by the storm, was blown towards a dangerous area of rocks. At the last moment, the wind changed, and the ship sailed into harbour.

People watching were amazed to see a dead body tied to the ship's steering wheel. There was no one else on deck. The ship had been steered to safety by the hand of a dead man!

The ship went aground in the harbour. Ropes and masts fell to the decks as she grounded. Then a very strange thing happened. A huge dog jumped from the deck and ran towards a nearby churchyard.

The rope used to tie the dead man to the wheel had cut him to the bone. A cross was tied to his wrists by a set of beads. A doctor said that the man had been dead for two days.

Shortly after the ship went aground, the storm died out.

From the *Daily News*, 8 August

STRANGE HAPPENINGS ON BOARD SHIP!

It is now known that the ship grounded in Whitby harbour sailed from Russia. It had a cargo of large wooden boxes filled with earth. These have now been taken ashore by a lawyer. He is acting for the owner, a foreign Count.

The RSPCA have been unable to find the dog that jumped from the ship.

It is now clear that the dead man found tied to the steering wheel was the captain. His diary was also found on board, and tells the amazing story of the voyage:

Captain's diary

6 July – We took a cargo of silver sand and fifty large boxes of earth. We set sail at noon, followed by a fresh east wind. There are nine people on board: five sailors, two mates, a cook and myself as captain.

13 July – The crew are unhappy for some reason. They seemed scared but will not say why.

14 July – I am worried about the crew. The mate asked them what was wrong. They would not answer and made the sign of the cross. The mate lost his temper and hit one of them. I expected to see a fight but the men did nothing. It is very strange.

16 July – One of the crew is missing. Nobody can explain this. The men are more frightened than ever. They say that there is something other than the cargo on board!

17 July – One of the men came to my cabin today. He was trembling with fear. He told me there was a strange man on board the ship. While he was on watch, he had sheltered behind the deck-house during a rainstorm. A tall thin man had come up the steps, walked along the deck and vanished. The sailor was so frightened I decided to have the ship searched. I wanted to stop a panic.

We made a thorough search of the ship but found nothing.

29 July – Another loss. The second mate has disappeared. The men are in a panic. We are all going to arm ourselves. We have run into storm, and are all tired. Another man lost during a storm.

30 July – We are getting nearer to England. All our sails are set. I went to sleep as I was too tired to keep going. The mate woke me. He told me that both the man on watch and the steersman are missing. There are now only myself, the mate and two hands left to work the ship.

1 August – We have had two days of fog. Not a sail could be seen. We are in the English Channel, so had hoped to get help from another ship. But the fog prevented this. I do not know what is going to happen to us.

2 August, midnight – I was woken up by a cry and rushed on deck. I met the first mate. He tells me another man has gone. Lord help us! The mate says we are now in the North Sea. The fog seems to move with us. Only God can now help us – and God seems to have left us.

3 August – At midnight I went to see the man at the wheel. When I got to it there was nobody there. I grabbed the wheel and shouted for the mate. He came rushing on deck and I could see that he had gone mad.

'I'm sure It is here,' he said. 'I know it now. I saw It last night. It was tall and thin and pale like a ghost. It was at the front of the ship looking out. I crept behind It. I stabbed with my knife, but the knife went clean through It.' As he spoke, he took out his knife and waved it in front of my face.

'But I know It is here,' he went on. 'I'll find It. It is in one of the boxes. I'll open them one by one. You work the wheel and leave it to me.' Then he went below. I saw him come out on deck again with a tool chest and a lamp. He is mad! He is stark raving mad. It is no use me trying to stop him!

Moments later I heard a scream which made my blood run cold. The mate came up on deck. He was a complete madman. His eyes rolled. His face was twisted with fear. 'Save me! Save me!' he cried. He stared around at the fog. Then he looked at me and said, 'He is there! I know the secret now. The sea will save me from him. You had better come too, Captain, before it is too late.' Before I could say a word he had thrown himself into the sea.

I see it all now. It was this madman who had got rid of the men one by one. And now he has killed himself. God help me! How am I going to explain these things when I get to port? When I get to port! Will I ever get there?

4 August – The fog is still all around the ship. There must be a sun, but it cannot break through. Last night I saw him! God forgive me, but the mate was right to jump overboard. It is better to die like a man in the blue water. But I am a captain and a captain must not leave his ship. I will tie my hands to the wheel. I will hold on to the cross which he cannot dare to touch. I must save my soul and my honour as a captain. I am getting weaker. The night is coming again. If we are wrecked, this log book may be found. God and the saints save me from this Demon. Help a poor sailor who is trying to do his best.·. . . (*End of the captain's diary.*)

The newspaper report (ending)

Nobody understands what all this means. Did the captain go insane? Did he kill the other sailors? The truth will never be known. The captain will be buried tomorrow.

7 Lucy in danger

Mina's diary

11 August, 3 a.m. – I am too upset to sleep. Something
terrible has happened. I awoke earlier in the night
and felt afraid. Lucy had disappeared. She was wearing only a nightdress so she could not have gone far.
I checked the house, but she was not there. I took a
heavy shawl and ran out. I knew she was sleep-walking
again.

The clock struck one as I ran through the empty
street. The moon was bright and full. But sometimes
it was hidden by black clouds. I saw the shape of
St Mary's church. I raced towards it. In the distance
I could see a white shape. A dark figure was crouched
over it. I ran as fast as I could but my feet seemed as
heavy as lead. Every joint in my body seemed rusty.
As I got nearer I saw there really was a long black
figure bending over the white shape.

'Lucy,' I shouted. A white face with red gleaming
eyes appeared. Then suddenly it vanished. I rushed
up to Lucy. I found she was still asleep. She was
breathing in long heavy gasps and she was shivering
with cold. I threw my shawl over her. I fastened it
with a safety pin, and led her back home.

Now Lucy is sleeping like a baby. The sun has risen
over the sea.
Same day, noon – All is well. Lucy slept till I woke her.

The adventure of the night does not seem to have harmed her. I saw that there were two little red holes in the skin of her throat. They looked like pinpricks. I said I was sorry for being so clumsy with the safety pin last night. She laughed and said she did not even feel it. Now we are both looking forward to a good night's rest.

12 August – During the night I was woken up twice. Lucy was trying to get out. Even in her sleep, she was trying to get out. She was upset to find the door shut. I had to force her to go back to bed. I woke with the dawn and heard the birds singing. Lucy woke too and seemed very much better.

13 August – I slept with the key on my wrist once again. I woke up during the night and found Lucy sitting up in bed. She was still asleep, but she was pointing at the window. I got up quickly. I pulled aside the blind and looked out. The moonlight was brilliant. It shone over the distant sea. It was all very beautiful. Then I saw a great bat. It kept coming and going in great circles. Once or twice it came quite close. But when it saw me it seemed to be frightened. It flitted away across the harbour. Then I saw it fly towards the church. When I came back from the window Lucy had lain down again. She was sleeping peacefully. She did not move again all night.

14 August – Last evening we went for a walk by St Mary's church. The sun was setting. It seemed to cover everything with a bright red light. We were silent for a while. Then suddenly Lucy began to talk quietly to herself.

'His red eyes again! They are just the same.'

It was such an odd thing to say! I turned round and saw a dark figure seated alone. The stranger seemed to have great eyes like burning flames – but it was just my eyes playing tricks. Lucy looked sad. I knew she must be thinking about that terrible night in the churchyard. She said she had a headache and went to bed early. I waited until she was asleep and then I went for a walk. I was feeling very sad about Jonathan.

When I came home I saw Lucy's head leaning out of the window. Her eyes were shut and she looked fast asleep. Seated nearby on the window sill was something that looked like a large bird. I ran quickly upstairs. When I entered the room she was moving back to her bed. She was still fast asleep. She was breathing heavily. She held her hand to her throat as if to protect it from the cold.

She looks paler than usual. There are lines below her eyes. I think she is ill again. Something is wrong with her and I wish I knew what it was. I noticed that the two safety pin marks were still on her throat. If they do not heal in a day or two, I shall ask the doctor to see them.

18 August – Lucy is ever so much better today. Last night she slept well. She did not disturb me once. The roses are coming back to her cheeks. She was so cheerful, I asked her if she had any dreams about the night she sleep-walked to the church.

She smiled and said, 'It did not seem like a dream. It all seemed so real. I was afraid of something. I remember passing through streets and over a bridge. A fish jumped up as I went by. I leaned over to look at it. I heard a lot of dogs howling. I remember something long and dark with red eyes. I seemed to be sinking into deep green water. There was a singing in my ears. My soul seemed to go out from my body. I

41

began to float into the air. Then there was a feeling of agony. But in the end I woke to find you shaking my body.'

I listened to her in amazement. Her story made me feel very worried, so I changed the subject.

I believe that she is a lot better now. It is as if some evil illness has suddenly gone away. Strange!

8 News of Jonathan

Mina's diary (continued)

19 August – Wonderful news! At last, there is word from Jonathan. He has been very ill. That is why he did not write before. Now Mr Hawkins has had a letter, he tells me. He says I should leave in the morning and go to Transylvania. I will meet Jonathan there. I will help to nurse him. Then I can bring him home. Mr Hawkins says we can get married out there. I have already mapped out my journey. I need take only one change of dress.

I cried all night over the letter. I am glad that Jonathan is alive, but some of the things in the letter are very worrying. So many strange things seem to be happening just recently.

Letter from a nurse in a hospital in Budapest

Dear Miss Mina Murray,   12 August
I am writing for Jonathan Harker. He is not strong
enough to write for himself yet. All the same he is
getting better, thanks to God. We have looked after
him for nearly six weeks. He was suffering from a
fever in his brains when he first came here. He asked
me to send you his love. He will need to have a few
weeks' rest in our hospital. Then he will be able to
return and be with you.

Yours, with good wishes,
Nurse Agatha

PS He is now asleep. I am just opening this letter to
tell you something else. He has told me all about you.
He says that you are soon to be his wife. May God
bless both of you!

But he has been through a terrible shock, our
doctor says. In his fever he shouted and screamed like
a madman. He talked of wolves, poison, blood,
ghosts, demons and all kinds of horrible things. Be
careful with him. He might become ill again. He is
only just strong enough to speak properly.

He is well looked after here. We like him very
much, as he is so kind and gentle. He is getting on well
and should make a full recovery in a few weeks' time.
But be careful with him for heaven's sake. I wish both
of you every happiness. May God be with you.

Letter from Mina Murray to Lucy Westen

My dearest Lucy,   Budapest, 24 August
I know you will want to hear all that has happened

since I left Whitby. Well, my dear, I got to Hull safely. Then I went by boat to Germany, and by train to the hospital here in Budapest.

My darling is so thin and pale. He is very weak. There is no life in his eyes and his face looks like that of a ghost. He is only a shadow of himself. He says he cannot remember what has happened to him. He has had some terrible shock. I am afraid he might go mad if he tries to remember it. Nurse Agatha tells me he talked and yelled all sorts of dreadful things when he was off his head. I wanted her to tell me what they were but she only crossed herself. She said the mad words of sick people were the secrets of God. But she said that he had done nothing to be ashamed of. She said that there was no other woman in his life, so I need not be jealous.

When he awoke, he told me he had been mad. He gave me a notebook and said the secret was written down there. He said I could read the book if I wanted. But he did not want me to read it out loud in case he went mad again. He said he did not think a husband and wife should have secrets from each other. I told him I did not want to upset him. I said I trusted him. I gave him the book back and said I did not want to read it at all.

Dear Lucy, we are to be married tomorrow! I must stop now. Jonathan is calling me. I hope you are better after your illness. I will see you again in four weeks' time. By then Jonathan will be well enough to travel.

Your ever loving,
Mina Murray (soon to be Mina HARKER!)

9 Renfield

Dr Seward's diary

(*Note: This man runs the lunatic asylum. He is worried about a lunatic called Renfield.*)

18 June – The case of Renfield is very strange. He is planning something, but I do not know what it is. I think he is a cruel person. He has some odd pets. His hobby is catching flies. He has so many I have had to tell him to get rid of them. To my surprise, he was not even angry. He thought for a moment then said: 'May I have three days? I shall clear them away.'

I must watch him.

25 June – Now he collects spiders! He has got several very big spiders in a box. He keeps feeding them with his flies.

1 July – His spiders are now as big a pest as his flies. So I told him to get rid of them. He looked very sad. I told him he could have three days to do this.

This man disgusts me at times. Once a horrid bluebottle buzzed into the room. It was filled with rotten food. He caught it. Then he held it between his finger and thumb and ate it. I told him off, but he said the fly was good to eat. He said it gave him life. I must watch to see how he gets rid of his spiders. I know he is up to something. He keeps a notebook full of numbers.

8 July – He has now managed to capture a sparrow. He feeds it on spiders and flies.

19 July – Renfield now has a whole flock of sparrows. At least his spiders and flies have almost gone.

Today he asked to see me. He wanted me to do him a favour. He said, 'Please give me a kitten, a nice playful kitten. I will play with it. I will teach it and feed it.'

I would not do this and he gave me a nasty look. The man is likely to turn into a murdering madman!

20 July – I went to see Renfield early this morning. He was putting sugar on the window sill. This is his way of trying to catch flies. I looked round for his birds but they were gone. He told me they had all flown away. There were a few feathers in the room. And there was a drop of blood on his pillow. I said nothing, but I told the keeper to tell me if anything odd happened.

11 a.m. – The keeper has just been to see me. Renfield has been sick. There were lots of feathers on the floor. It was horrible. 'I think that he has eaten his birds,' said the keeper. 'I think he just took them and ate them raw!'

11 p.m. – I gave Renfield a sleeping drug and took away his notebook. It seems this madman wants to eat up as many living things as he can. I believe he keeps count of the number of living things he has eaten. It is all very strange!

26 August – Renfield escaped last night. The last two days he had been very quiet. He had thrown away his spiders and had just sat staring into space.

Last night, some of the keepers ran into my room. They told me the lunatic had escaped. They led me into the grounds of that big house nearby and there we saw him. He was leaning against the chapel door. He seemed to be talking to somebody. We crept up to him very carefully. I heard him say, 'I am here to do what you want, Master. I am your slave and you will reward me. I have worshipped you for a long time.'

When we grabbed him, he fought like a tiger. He is extremely strong. He is more like a wild animal than a man. I never saw a lunatic so angry. We put him in a strait-jacket and chained him to a wall in the padded room. His cries are dreadful but we dare not unchain him yet. We feel he is planning some form of murder.

Just now he spoke for the first time since we captured him.

'I shall be patient, Master,' he said. 'It is coming – coming – coming!'

10 Lucy gets worse

Lucy Westen's diary

24 August, London – I must keep writing everything down like Mina does. Then we can have long talks when we meet again. I wonder when it will be. I wish she was with me now, for I feel so unhappy. Last night I had a dream. It was just like the one I had at Whitby. Perhaps it is the change of air. Perhaps London does not suit me. Everything seems dark and

horrid. I am frightened. I feel so weak and worn out.
When Arthur saw me, he was very worried. I wonder
if I can sleep in my mother's room tonight?
25 August – Another bad night. Mother does not want
me to sleep in her room. She is very sick herself and
does not want to frighten me. I fell asleep but the clock
woke me at twelve. There was a sort of scratching and
flapping at the window. That is all I can remember,
so I suppose I must have fallen asleep again. I had
more bad dreams. I wish I could remember them. This
morning I am very weak. My face is pale, and my
throat hurts me. Perhaps there is something wrong
with my lungs. I must try to be cheerful when Arthur
comes. I do not want to upset him.

Letter from Arthur Holmwood to Dr Seward

My dear Jack,   31 August
I want you to do me a favour. Lucy is ill. We do not
know what the illness is, but she looks terrible and is
getting worse every day. I dare not tell her mother of
my fears. The old lady has a weak heart and will soon
die. I am sure that something is wrong with Lucy's
mind. Could you come to London tomorrow? I am
really desperate for Lucy's sake. Please come!

I will not be able to meet you in London because
my father is ill. I must go and see him before he dies.

Arthur

Letter from Dr Seward to Arthur Holmwood

My dear old fellow,   2 September
I am sorry you could not meet me in London. I hope
your father gets better. I examined Miss Westen and

I am rather puzzled. I have tested her blood. It is quite normal, but she seems extremely weak. I am going to ask my old Professor to come over from Amsterdam. His name is Van Helsing. He is perhaps the most brilliant doctor in Europe. He is also a very kind man, but he cannot speak very good English. I will stay with Lucy until this man arrives.

Yours always,
Jack Seward

11 Van Helsing

(*Note: Van Helsing is one of the world's greatest doctors. He knows all about vampires, but he does not tell anyone what he suspects. He does not want to frighten them. Also, he knows they would not believe him. They would laugh at him, or think he was mad.*)

Dr Seward's diary

7 September – As soon as Van Helsing got here, we went into Lucy's room together.

The blind was down. I went over and lifted it gently. Van Helsing stepped towards the bed as softly as he could.

The morning sunlight poured into the room. The Professor gave a deep hiss and stepped back in horror.

'Good God!' he said. He lifted his hand and pointed to the bed. His face was as white as ashes. I felt my knees begin to tremble.

There on the bed lay poor Lucy, the dear girl I had wanted to marry. She was more horribly white than I had ever seen her before. Even her lips were white and the gums seemed to have shrunk back from her teeth. She looked like a corpse. There were two small pinpricks on her neck.

'Quick!' said Van Helsing. 'Bring the brandy.' I ran to the dining room and came back with a bottle. He poured a few drops between her poor white lips. Then we rubbed her hands and wrists and heart.

After a few moments of waiting, he said, 'It is not too late. The heart beats but it is weak.'

He dipped into his bag and brought out the instruments needed for a blood transfusion. I pulled up my shirt sleeve. Soon my blood was pumping through the girl's veins.

Lucy slept for most of the day and when she awoke she seemed much stronger.

10 September – Lucy is making great progress. A big parcel from abroad came for Van Helsing. He opened it and took out some flowers.

He said to Lucy, 'These are for you. They are as good as any strong medicine. I shall put them on your window sill. I shall make a pretty chain of some of them and hang them round your neck, so that you sleep well.'

Lucy looked at them and laughed. 'Oh Professor! What nonsense! These flowers are only wild garlic!'

Van Helsing stood up and became serious. 'I never joke,' he snapped. 'You must do as you are told. Your life is in danger.' He saw that Lucy was frightened, so he changed his voice. 'Oh, do not be afraid, little miss! I only get angry for your own good.'

I watched the Professor spread garlic all over the bedroom. He shut the windows. Then he rubbed the windows and door with the flowers. I was amazed.

'This is very strange,' I said. 'It looks as if you are trying to keep out an evil spirit.'

'Perhaps I am,' he answered quietly. He began to fix the garlic round Lucy's neck. 'Take care you do not move it,' he said. 'And even if the room feels stuffy, you must not open the window or door.'

Lucy Westen's diary

17 September – Seven days and nights of peace. I am getting so strong again that I hardly know myself. I feel as though I have just been through a long nightmare. I feel I have woken up to the fresh air and sunshine. Since Dr Van Helsing has been with me, all my bad dreams seem to have gone. All the noises that used to scare me out of my wits have stopped. There is no more flapping against the windows. I do not hear the harsh sounds and distant voices that seemed to rule my life. I am no longer afraid of sleeping. I do not even try to keep awake. I have grown to like the garlic, and a fresh boxful arrives for me each day from Holland.

Van Helsing has to go back to Amsterdam tonight. But there is no need for me to be watched. I am well enough to be left alone. I hope Arthur's father soon gets better. I miss Arthur so much. But I am sure I can now manage without my good friend Van Helsing. He fell asleep twice in his chair during the night, but I was not at all afraid.

12 The victims

Dr Seward's diary

17 September, The asylum – I was reading a book when
the door suddenly burst open. Renfield, the lunatic,
stood there. He was snarling. I was amazed. No patient
has ever broken into my study before. He charged
straight at me. He had a dinner knife in his hand and
I knew he was dangerous. I tried to keep the desk
between us but he jumped over it. He cut my wrist
with his knife. I punched him to the floor and waited
for him to attack me again. My wrist was bleeding.
It made a little pool on the floor.

Renfield was suddenly quiet, and I began to
bandage my wound. Some men rushed in and we
made a circle around the lunatic. What he was doing
was disgusting. He was lying on the floor and he was
licking up my blood like a dog. He did not struggle as
we took him away. But he kept saying these words
again and again: 'Blood is life! Blood is life!'

Diary of Lucy Westen

*(Note: Van Helsing had to go back to Holland for two days.
He sent a telegram to Dr Seward telling him to go to Lucy's
home. He told everybody to watch Lucy night and day. Lucy's
mother promised to do this until Van Helsing gets back.*

Lucy's mother is an old woman who knows nothing at all about vampires.)

17 September – I simply must write down what happened tonight. I feel I am dying of weakness. I hardly have the strength to write. But it must be done, even if I die in doing it.

I went to bed as usual and placed the flowers round my neck as Van Helsing told me to do. I soon fell asleep.

Later, I was woken by a flapping noise at the window. I was not afraid, but I wished that Dr Seward or Van Helsing were near. I tried to sleep but I could not. It seemed safer to stay awake.

I opened the door and called out: 'Is anybody there?' There was no answer. I did not want to wake my mother, so I closed the door again. Then I heard a sort of howl outside in the bushes. It was like a dog's but more fierce and deeper. I went to the window and looked out. I could see nothing except a big bat. It had been banging its wings against the window. I went back to bed again, but somehow felt I did not want to go to sleep.

Soon the door opened. My mother looked in. She sat down beside me. 'I was worried about you,' she said. 'I just came to see if you were all right!'

I was afraid she would catch cold. I told her to sleep with me. She came into bed and lay down beside me.

Then the flapping and battering at the window began again. My mother was frightened and cried out. 'What is that?' I tried to calm her nerves but I could hear her poor old heart. It was beating madly. There was a low howl again from the bushes. Suddenly there was a crash at the window and broken glass fell to the floor. The window blind was swept back by a gust of wind. There stood a huge grey wolf!

My mother cried out in fear. She hit out wildly. In doing this she tore away the flowers from my neck. She shook her hand at the wolf. Then she gasped and fell back. Her head banged against mine. I tried to move but I was trapped by her body. I knew her heart had stopped beating and I was frightened. I could hear the wolf howling through the open window. Then I saw hundreds of specks of bright light. They swirled about like coloured dust. I felt as though a spell had been placed upon me. I must have fainted.

Those specks are coming back! I can hear the wolf howling again. I will hide this paper so that they will find it when they lay my body out. Good-bye, dear Arthur, if I do not survive this night. God keep you, dear, and God help me!

13 Lucy's struggle

Dr Seward's diary

18 September – I was given a telegram from Van Helsing early this morning. I saw from the date it had taken twenty-four hours to reach me. I drove at once to London and arrived while it was still early. I rang the bell, but there was no answer. Every door and window was closed, so I went back to the front porch. As I did so, I heard the rapid pit-pat of a horse-drawn carriage. Then I saw Van Helsing running up the path.

When he saw me he gasped out, 'Have you only just arrived? How is she? Are we too late? Did you not get my telegram?'

I told him his telegram had only arrived early that morning. I had not lost a minute in coming here. I told him I could get no one to answer the door.

He took off his hat and said sadly, 'Then we are too late. God's will be done.'

But then he seemed to recover his hope. He said, 'Come on. There is not a second to lose!'

We broke down the back door and went into the kitchen. The servants were lying on the floor. They must have been drugged. We opened the door to Lucy's room. Our faces were white and our hands were trembling.

How shall I describe what we saw? On the bed lay Lucy and her mother. The old woman's white face was frozen in a mask of terror. By her side lay Lucy. The white flowers had been torn from her neck and lay on her mother's breast. The girl's throat was bare. It showed the two little pinpricks we had noticed before. But they now looked horribly white and ugly. The Professor did not say a word at first.

Then he bent over the bed, and said, 'It is not too late! Quick! Quick! Bring the brandy!'

We forced some brandy down her throat. Then Van Helsing took out his instruments for a blood transfusion. He stopped suddenly.

'What's wrong?' I said.

'I must have fresh blood,' he said. 'You are too

tired, and so am I. We cannot use the servants because they have been drugged. What can we do?'

A voice came from outside the door.

'What about me, then?'

It was Quincey Morris! It was the American who had once proposed to Lucy!

'What brought you here?' I cried.

'I got a telegram from Arthur. His father is still very sick, and Arthur can't leave him. He asked me to look after Lucy. I guess I'm just in time. What are we waiting for?'

Van Helsing was very happy. 'A brave man's blood is the best thing on this earth,' he said. He began the transfusion. After the transfusion, we took Quincey downstairs. We gave him some coffee. Lucy was still unconscious, but Van Helsing and I made her more comfortable. As we did this, we noticed a piece of paper in her bed. Van Helsing read it and then handed it to me.

I looked at the Professor. After a while, I asked him, 'In God's name, what does it all mean? Is she mad? What sort of horrible danger is it?'

Van Helsing out out his hand and took the paper. He said, 'Do not worry about it now. Forget it for the present. You will understand it soon, but not yet. You must arrange for the burial of the poor old lady who has died.

On my way out I saw Quincey Morris again. He was sending a telegram to Arthur. It was to tell him that Mrs Westen was dead, and Lucy was very ill but would get better.

Quincey said to me, 'Jack, when you get back, could I speak to you?' I nodded and went out.

Later – When I got back to the house, Quincey was

waiting for me. We went in to Lucy's room. She was still unconscious. Van Helsing was sitting in a chair. He told us we were not needed for the present. So we went into the breakfast room, and Quincey began to speak about Lucy.

'Jack,' he said. 'I don't wish to stick my nose in where I'm not wanted, but I did once love that girl. I'm worried about her. You say that you and Van Helsing have given her your blood as well as me?'

'That's right,' I replied.

'And Arthur has done the same, hasn't he? Last time I saw him he looked very weak. And when I saw Lucy, she looked dreadful. It reminded me of the time I was in South America. One of my horses had a cut on her neck. During the night, one of those big bats called vampires got at it. Next morning the horse was so weak I had to shoot it. Tell me, Jack how long has Lucy been like this?'

'About a fortnight.'

'A fortnight!' he said. 'The poor girl has had the blood of four strong men pumped into her veins. I want to know where that blood has gone.'

I shook my head. 'I just don't know. Van Helsing is very worried about it and I am at my wit's end. I can't even guess. All I know is this. We have to watch her every minute of the day and all through the night.'

Quincey held out his hand. 'You can count on my help,' he said. 'You tell me what to do, and I'll do it.'

Lucy woke later in the morning. The first thing she did was to feel for the piece of paper. To my surprise, the Professor had put it back so as not to upset her. When she saw Van Helsing and myself, she smiled. Then she gave a loud cry and put her thin hands up to her pale face. She had suddenly remembered the death of her mother. We tried to comfort her, but she wept all through the afternoon.

As it got dark, she fell into a doze. Then a very odd thing happened. Whilst still asleep she took the paper from her breast and tore it in two. Van Helsing stepped over and took the pieces from her. All the same, she went on tearing as though the paper was still in her hands. Finally, she opened her hands and moved them as if throwing away the pieces. Van Helsing seemed surprised. He frowned but said nothing.

19 September – Lucy slept badly last night. In the morning she looked terribly weak. Her open mouth showed her gums were pale. Her teeth look very much longer and sharper. Arthur has come back. He is very upset. Lucy is too weak. The shock has been too great. I fear the end will come tomorrow. The poor child will not recover. God help us all.

14 Death

Letter from Mina Harker to Lucy Westen

(*Note: Mina does not know that Lucy is very ill.*)

My dearest Lucy,   18 September
We have just arrived in Exeter. Jonathan is much better, but we received a terrible piece of news. Mr Hawkins has died. He was the man Jonathan worked

for, and we loved him as a father. The poor old man left his fortune and business to Jonathan. The funeral will be tomorrow. We will of course be going to it. I hope to see you as soon as possible.
Your loving,
Mina Harker

Dr Seward's diary

20 September – I am sick and tired of this miserable world. I would not give a damn if I died tomorrow.

Last night, Lucy's face looked terrible. Her teeth looked longer and sharper. I sat down by her and she moved about in her sleep. There came a sort of dull flapping at the window. I went over to it softly. I peeped out by the corner of the blind. There was a full moonlight, and I could see that the noise was made by a great bat. It kept striking the window with its wings. When I came back to my seat, I found that Lucy had moved in her sleep. She had torn the garlic flowers away from her throat. I put them back and sat watching her.

At six o'clock Van Helsing came to take over. Arthur had fallen asleep and Van Helsing let him sleep on. When he saw Lucy's face I heard him gasp. He said to me in a whisper: 'Draw up the blind. I want light!'

Then he bent down. His face almost touched Lucy's. He examined her carefully. He took away the flowers and lifted the silk handkerchief from her throat. As he did so he jumped back. I heard him cry 'My God!'

I bent over and looked too. I felt cold all over. The wounds on Lucy's throat had completely vanished.

Van Helsing stared at her for a whole five minutes.

Then he turned to me and said quickly, 'She is dying. It will not be long now. Wake poor Arthur. I promised he should see her before she dies.'

I went to the dining room and woke Arthur. When we came into the room, Lucy opened her eyes.

She whispered softly, 'Arthur! Oh, my love, I am so glad you have come!' He was stooping to kiss her when Van Helsing stopped him, 'No,' he whispered, 'not yet! Hold her hand. It will comfort her more.'

So Arthur took her hand and knelt beside her. Gradually her eyes closed and she went to sleep. For a while her breasts moved softly up and down. Her breath came and went like a tired child's.

And then came the strange change. I had noticed this happen the night before. Her breathing grew loud and heavy. The mouth opened. The pale gums were pulled back. This made her teeth look longer and sharper than ever. She awoke but her eyes had a strange faraway look. When she spoke, her voice was soft and frightening. I had never heard her talk like this before.

'Arthur!' she said. 'Oh, my love, I am so glad you have come! Kiss me!'

Arthur leaned over. He was just about to kiss her when Van Helsing sprang into action. He grabbed Arthur by the neck and actually threw him across the room. I would never have guessed that Van Helsing had such strength.

'It is more than your life is worth!' he said, 'You must not kiss her.'

And he stood between them like a lion at bay.

Arthur was amazed. He just stood there watching in silence. I kept my eyes fixed on Lucy, and so did Van Helsing. We saw a look of rage pass like a shadow over her face. The sharp teeth bit hard together. Then her eyes closed and she breathed heavily.

Very shortly after, she opened her eyes. She held out her poor thin hand. She caught hold of Van Helsing's large brown hand and kissed it. 'My true friend,' she said. 'My true friend and his! Oh God, save you both.'

Van Helsing spoke to Arthur. 'Come on,' he said. 'Take her hand in yours and kiss her just once – on the forehead.'

Their eyes met instead of their lips.

Lucy's eyes closed. Her breathing became loud and heavy. Then all at once it stopped.

'It is all over,' said Van Helsing. 'She is dead!'

I took Arthur by the arm and led him away to another room. There he sat down and covered his face with his hands. He sobbed in a way that nearly broke my heart to see. I went back to the room and saw Van Helsing looking down at poor Lucy. His face was grim. Some change had come over her body. She did not look so pale now. It seemed as though death had made her more beautiful.

I stood beside Van Helsing and said, 'Ah, poor girl. There is peace for her at last. It is the end!'

He turned to me, and said with a strange look, 'You are wrong. It is only the beginning!'

I asked him what he meant. He only shook his head. 'We can do nothing yet. Wait and see.'

15 The burial

Dr Seward's diary

21 September – Lucy will be buried tomorrow with her
mother. Van Helsing, Arthur and myself went into the
room. We went to see how the undertaker had laid
her out. We were all amazed by her beauty.

Arthur fell trembling to his knees and said to me,
'Jack, is she really dead?'

I told him that she was in fact dead. Van Helsing
then took us aside.

'Listen to me,' he said. 'Lucy is truly dead and can
never come to life again. Tomorrow, before nightfall
I would like you to help me. Forgive me for seeming
to be clumsy. You must prepare yourselves for a
shock. I want to cut off her head and take out her
heart.'

'No!' yelled Arthur.

'That's out of the question,' I said. 'How can you
say such a thing?'

Van Helsing turned to face me. 'Are you shocked,
Jack? You are a doctor. I have seen you operate on
the living and the dead. Your hand never trembled.'

'But why?' I asked. 'Why do it at all? The girl is
dead. Why cut up her poor body into pieces? There is
no need for it.'

Van Helsing put his arms around the shoulders of
Arthur and myself. 'Do not think I am cruel. You

were amazed and horrified when I would not let Arthur kiss his love, even though she was dying. But did you see how she thanked me and kissed my hand afterwards? I know things that you do not know. Will you trust me?'

Arthur shook his head. 'I trust and respect you, Van Helsing,' he said. 'You are a good and a noble man. But I still love this girl. I will not allow her poor dead body to be cut up. I'm sorry.'

Then the poor fellow burst into tears. Van Helsing nodded. 'Very well,' he said. 'But we will all have to suffer a great deal in the next few days.'

22 September – I slept on a sofa in Arthur's room last night. Van Helsing did not go to bed at all. He walked about as if guarding the house. He was never out of sight of the room where Lucy lay in her coffin. She was covered with the wild garlic flowers, mixed together with lilies and roses. The flowers made a strange and powerful smell.

Mina Harker's diary

22 September – We went to London for the funeral and burial of dear Mr Hawkins. It was all very sad because we both loved the old man. Later, after nightfall, he went to a small café and sat down. Suddenly I felt Jonathan clutch my arm. He said under his breath, 'My God!'

I am always worried that Jonathan's madness may return, so I turned to him quickly. I asked him what was the matter.

Jonathan was white-faced. His eyes seemed to stand out of his head in amazement and terror. He was staring at a tall, thin man with a sharp nose. The man had a black moustache and a pointed beard. He was staring at a pretty girl and did not notice us. I looked closely at this man. He had a hard, cruel face, with big white teeth and extremely red lips. Jonathan kept staring at him. I asked him again what the matter was. Jonathan seemed to think I knew who the man was.

'Do you see who it is?' he asked.

'No, dear,' I replied. 'I don't know him. Who is it?'

'It is the man himself!'

Poor Jonathan was terrified. If I had not been there to lean on, I think he would have fallen. He kept staring at the man. Suddenly the girl left and the dark man followed her. Jonathan watched him go.

Then he said, as if to himself, 'I believe it is the Count, but he has grown younger, my God! Oh, my God!'

We walked through the streets, then sat down on a park bench. It was a very hot night and the seat was comfortable. After a few minutes, Jonathan's eyes closed. He went into a sleep. I did not dare disturb him. In twenty minutes he woke up. I was amazed by his cheerfulness.

'Why, Mina,' he said, 'I have been asleep! Do forgive me for being so rude. Let's have a cup of tea somewhere.'

I knew then that he had forgotten about the stranger. I am extremely worried by all this. It is time to open the parcel with Jonathan's diary inside. I must find out what happened to him in Transylvania. *Later* – More bad news. It never seems to end! I have just been given a telegram from Dr Seward. It says that Mrs Westen and Lucy are both dead. A man called Van Helsing is to visit me to ask some questions about Lucy.

Poor Mrs Westen! Poor Lucy! They have gone and will never come back to us! And poor, poor Arthur. He has lost such sweetness out of his life. God help us all.

Dr Seward's diary

22 September – Van Helsing has been acting strangely. I am worried that the old man may be going mad. He turned white and then purple during the burial. He looked very ill. Then afterwards, he laughed when he was in the carriage. He laughed till tears streamed down his face. I told him to take a sleeping tablet before he went completely mad. Suddenly he seemed to get better.

'You do not understand, Jack,' he said. 'I laugh because I do not want to suffer too much. I laugh because the undertaker and the priests and the people at the funeral are being made fools of. I laugh because I know something they do not.'

I did not argue with him. He is a good man. He will recover with a few days' rest. I only hope he does not upset Mina when he visits her to ask about Lucy.

Poor Lucy! Now she is dead. She lies in a tomb with the rest of her family. It is a tomb in a lonely church-yard not far away from London. At least she lies in a place where the air is fresh and the sun rises over Hampstead Heath. It is a place where wild flowers grow.

So now I can finish this diary. Only God knows if I will ever begin another.

16 The white lady

The *Westminster Gazette*, 25 September

(*Note: The story is told by a reporter for a London newspaper. He does not know anything about vampires or about Lucy's death.*)

A HAMPSTEAD MYSTERY

Strange things have been happening in Hampstead. Small children have been disappearing from the Heath while playing. They come back after a short while, but they are all too young to explain what has happened to them. They all disappear during the late evening. One of them said that a 'white lady' had taken him for a walk.

There could be something very evil in all this. Some of the children have been hurt in the throat. The cuts look as if a rat or a small dog has made them. The police have asked parents not to let their children play on the Heath. They would like more information about this 'white lady'.

The *Westminster Gazette*, 26 September

THE HAMPSTEAD HORROR

We have just been given some news that another child went missing last night. He was found late in the morning under a bush at the Shooter's Hill side of

Hampstead Heath. (This is a wilder part of the Heath which few people visit.) The child had the same tiny cuts on the throat and was very weak. When he was better, he told the same story about the 'white lady' who had taken him for a walk.

Mina Harker's diary

24 September – Last night I read Jonathan's diary. Poor Jonathan! How he must have suffered. Was it all in his mind? I wonder if it was really true! Was it brain fever? I dare not ask Jonathan. It might drive him mad again. But his story seems to fit together. The terrible Count *was* coming to London. I can see why Jonathan wants to forget. The idea is too terrible even to think about.

25 September – Dr Van Helsing came to see me. What a strange meeting! I simply cannot believe what I heard. My head is spinning round.

He arrived at half past two. He said he was very worried about Lucy's death. He asked if he could read some of the letters she wrote to me about her sleep-walking. Of course I agreed. Then I asked him for some advice about my husband and his strange dreams I gave him the diary to read. The Professor took it off into a quiet room. He came back after half an hour, and took me by the hands.

'The story is true,' he said. 'There is nothing wrong with your husband's heart or his brain.'

I am very happy to know that at least my husband is not mad. But to think of that dreadful creature in London! It makes my flesh creep!

Jonathan Harker's diary

26 September – I never thought I would write in this
diary again, but the time has come. When I got home
last night I met Van Helsing. He told me that I had
not dreamed up all those things that happened in
Castle Dracula. Now I feel like a new man. I am
happy to know that I am not mad. I am no longer
afraid, not even of the Count. So he has managed to
get to London. It *was* him I saw in the café. How has
he got younger?

Van Helsing had to catch a morning train. I went
with him to the station and talked to him at the train
window. As he waited for the train to start, he turned
over one of last night's newspapers. Then his eyes
suddenly seemed to see something in one of them. It
was the *Westminster Gazette* – I knew it by the colour.
He grew quite white. He read something and groaned
out loud. 'My God! My God! So soon! So soon!'

Just then the whistle blew and the train moved off.
He suddenly awoke from this day-dream. He leaned
out of the window and waved his hand.

He called out, 'Give my love to Madam Mina. I
shall write as soon as I can.'

Dr Seward's diary

(*Note: He is at the lunatic asylum. The asylum is next to
Count Dracula's estate.*)

26 September – I did not think I would have to write in
this diary again. Everything seemed to have come to
some sort of end. Lucy was dead. Renfield had become
much less violent, and was now catching spiders and
flies again. Arthur seemed to be getting over his

broken heart. As for myself, I was back to normal work. Then, about half past five, Van Helsing rushed into my study. He pushed a copy of last night's *Westminster Gazette* into my hand.

'What do you think of that?' he asked. Then he stood back and folded his arms.

I did not know what to look for and said so. Van Helsing pointed out a story about children being attacked in Hampstead. It did not mean much to me until I reached a part where it talked about the tiny little holes in their throats. I looked up.

'Well?' said Van Helsing.

'It is like poor Lucy's,' I said.

'And what do you make of it?' he asked.

I thought for a while, then said, 'Whatever attacked her has also attacked them'

'That is only half true,' he said.

I was puzzled. 'What do you mean, Professor?' I asked.

Van Helsing took a deep breath. 'Do you mean to tell me that you have no idea at all?'

I shook my head. He stepped over and sat down beside me.

He went on, 'You are a clever man, Jack, and a very good doctor. But you have no imagination. Tell me, do you believe in mind-reading? Do you believe that people can put their own ideas into the minds of animals and other creatures? Do you believe in things from outer space? Do you believe in hypnotism?'

'I believe in hypnotism,' I replied, 'but not the rest. That's all mumbo-jumbo.'

'Jack!' he cried. 'Science is wonderful but the world is still full of mystery. The scientist of today would have been burned as a witch in times gone by. Or he would have been treated as a god. But there are still things we cannot explain. Why did Lucy die in spite of having four men's blood in her veins? Why are there huge bats in South America that drink the blood of cattle? Why do these bats come down upon sleeping sailors and drink them dry of blood?'

'Good God, Professor!' I said, jumping up. 'Do you mean to tell me that Lucy was bitten by such a bat? Do you think there is such a thing here in London today?'

Van Helsing waved his hand for silence and went on.

'Can you tell me why a tortoise lives for hundreds of years? Why do some men believe it is possible to live for ever? Can you tell me how an Indian wise man can die and be buried, then be dug up a year later, get up from his coffin and live again?'

By now my head was spinning. I had to stop him. My head was dizzy with all these questions.

'Professor,' I said. 'What is it you want to tell me?

Van Helsing folded his arms. 'I want you to believe,' he said.

'To believe what?'

'The holes made in the throats of the children. You think they were made by the thing that attacked Lucy, don't you?'

'I suppose so.'

He stood up. 'Then you are wrong. It is worse, far worse.'

'In God's name, what do you mean?' I cried.

He threw himself into a chair and covered his face with his hands.

'They were made by Lucy herself!' he said.

For a moment I was too angry to speak. It was as

though he was spitting on the dead body of poor Lucy. I smashed my fist on the table and rose to my feet.

'Dr Van Helsing, you've gone mad!'

The old man shook his head sadly. 'I wish I was,' he said. 'Tonight I will prove to you that it is true. If you have the courage, we will visit Lucy's tomb. Well?'

Of course I had to agree. I was sorry to have lost my temper with Van Helsing. Yet I knew I was going to see something very horrible.

It was already dark by the time we set off. As we got nearer the church, we met fewer and fewer people. Soon we were the only people around. The Professor took a key and opened the creaky door. He asked me to enter first. Then he fumbled in his bag. He took out a piece of candle and a box of matches. In day-time the tomb looked very frightening, even when covered with flowers. Now, the flowers were dead and covered with spiders and beetles. The very stones smelled of death. Van Helsing took out a screw-driver.

'What are you going to do?' I asked.

'Open the coffin. We will find out the truth.'

He took out the screws and lifted the lid. I stepped back. I expected a rush of gas from a rotted corpse. The Professor held the candle above the coffin and told me to look.

I stepped near and looked inside. The coffin was empty!

It surprised me, but not Van Helsing. 'Are you satisfied now?' he asked.

'No,' I said. 'Some body-snatchers have been at work.'

'Very well,' he laughed. 'We must have more proof. Come with me.'

We left the tomb and waited at the side of the churchyard. It was a dark and lonely wait. Three hours went by. I was cold and angry. I felt the Professor had made a fool of me.

Suddenly, I turned round. I thought I saw something. It looked like a white streak moving between two dark trees. It was going towards the tomb. I ran off to follow it. When I got to the spot, I saw the Professor. He was holding a tiny child in his arms. He saw me, and held it out.

'Are you satisfied now?'

'No,' I said.

'Look at the child!' snapped Van Helsing.

'I can see the child, but who brought it here? And is it wounded?'

He held the child up to the moonlight. There was no mark on its throat this time.

'You see!' I cried. 'I was right. There's nothing in all this.'

'Only because we were just in time,' said the Professor.

We had to decide what to do with the child now. It clearly needed to be taken to hospital. But we thought the police would laugh at our story about vampires. They would put us in prison for child-stealing. So we took the child to the edge of the Heath to wait for a policeman to come. We placed the child on the grass, well in view, and ran off to our carriage and drove back home.

I am too tired to sleep. Van Helsing says we must make another visit to the tomb! What a waste of time!

72

17 A stake in the heart

Dr Seward's diary (continued)

27 September – It was two o'clock in the afternoon when we arrived outside the tomb for the second time. I felt unhappy about the whole business. We were breaking the law. We were risking years in prison. And I felt it was all so useless. It was a disgusting idea to open the coffin of a woman who had been dead for a week. Since the coffin had been empty yesterday, it seemed mad to open it up again. I swore under my breath as Van Helsing opened up the coffin once again. And then a shock of surprise shot through me.

There lay Lucy! She looked as fresh and as beautiful as she had done on the night of the funeral. She looked so lovely I could not believe she was dead. The lips were even redder than before and there was a blush on her cheeks.

'Is this a dream?' I asked.

'Do you believe me now?' said the Professor. As he spoke, he pulled back the dead lips and showed the white teeth.

'See,' he went on. 'See, they are even sharper than before. These are the teeth that bit the throats of the little children. Now do you believe me?'

But I would not believe him. 'She may have been placed here last night.'

'Indeed? Who by?'

'I don't know.'

'Look,' said the Professor. 'She has been dead one week. She has not begun to rot. She was bitten by the vampire. She is now un-dead. We must kill her.' He looked at me and smiled. 'Now you believe me, don't you?'

'All right!' I said. 'How will you do this bloody work?'

'I shall cut off her head and fill her mouth with garlic. Then I shall drive a stake through her body.' It made me shudder to think of chopping up the body of a woman I had once loved. But I was not so disgusted as I might have been. I was beginning to be frightened of this un-dead creature.

But Van Helsing put away his knives and the stake. 'First we must make sure Arthur believes what we say about Lucy. Otherwise he will hate us for ever. We will come back in two or three days' time. We will return with Arthur and that brave American called Quincey Morris.'

Note written by Van Helsing to Jack Seward

Dear Jack,   27 September
Tonight I will go alone to watch Lucy's tomb. I will place garlic and a cross at the entrance of the tomb. I want her to stay inside tonight so she will be more anxious to leave tomorrow.

Van Helsing

Dr Seward's diary

28 September – I feel much better after a good night's

sleep. Yesterday I almost believed all that nonsense Van Helsing talked. Now I realize he is going mad. I must watch him very carefully.

29 September, morning – Van Helsing told Arthur and Quincey of his plan. Arthur was horrified.

'You want us to go to Lucy's tomb?'

'Yes,' said the Professor.

'And what then?' Arthur asked.

'We enter the tomb,' said the Professor.

'Are you mad!' said Arthur, staring at him. 'What are we going to do when we are inside?'

'Open the coffin,' said the Professor.

'WHAT!' shouted Arthur. He was almost foaming at the mouth.

'Lucy is not dead.'

Arthur jumped to his feet. 'Good God!' he shouted. 'What do you mean? Has there been a mistake? Has she been buried alive?'

'She is un-dead.'

'What the devil are you talking about?' shouted Arthur.

Quincey Morris spoke. 'Cool down, Arthur,' he said. 'Let's go with him and find out what it's all about. We've got nothing to lose, have we?'

It was just before midnight when we reached the tomb. The coffin was empty, so we sat down to wait. It was a beautiful night. The air was fresh and sweet and the clouds could be seen in the moonlight. Arthur chewed his fingernails. He was very nervous. Quincey bit his lips. Van Helsing spread garlic at the entrance of the tomb. He said that he wanted to stop anybody entering. Far away, dogs were howling in the night.

There was a long spell of silence. Suddenly the Professor hissed and pointed. Far down the avenue of trees, we saw a white figure. It was coming nearer. It was a white figure with something dark at its breast. The figure stopped. A ray of moonlight fell upon a dark-haired woman. She was dressed in funeral clothes. We could not see the face at first. The woman was bent over a fair-haired child.

There was a sharp little cry. We were about to rush forward but Van Helsing stopped us. The white figure came towards us again. I could hear Arthur gasp and my heart turned cold. We saw the face of Lucy Westen. But how she had changed! Her sweetness had turned to cruelty. She had the face of a beautiful witch. Van Helsing stepped forward and we followed. He held up the lantern. We could see that her lips were red with fresh blood. The stream had trickled over her chin and stained the whiteness of her funeral clothes.

We shivered with horror. I could see by the lamplight that even Van Helsing was trembling. Arthur would have fallen if I had not caught hold of him.

When Lucy – I must call her that only because it looked like her – saw us, she drew back with an angry growl. She was like a cat taken by surprise. Then she looked at us. Her eyes were wild and full of hell-fire. I hated this monster. Her eyes blazed with cruelty and she smiled. She showed those horrible teeth. Oh, God, how it made me shudder! She flung the child to the floor and stood growling over it. She looked like a dog with a bone. The child gave a cry and lay there moaning. Then this hellish creature opened her arms and moved towards Arthur. He fell back and hid his face in his hands.

'Come to me, Arthur,' she cried. 'Leave the others and come with me. My arms are waiting for you.

Come, and we can rest together. Come, my husband, come!'

There was something horribly sweet in her voice. It was like the sound of glass when you tap it with a spoon. It rang through our brains as if to hypnotize us. Arthur seemed in a trance. He moved towards her. His arms were wide open. The evil creature was about to grab him when Van Helsing sprang forward. He held a cross between them. The white lady jumped back and tried to escape into the tomb.

But the garlic held her back. She turned to face us. I have never seen such ugliness! Snakes seemed to crawl across her face. Her blood-filled mouth opened and she spat upon the grass. Van Helsing turned to Arthur.

'Will you let me do my work?'

'Yes!' said Arthur. He fell to his knees in despair. Van Helsing made a gap in the garlic and the evil creature fled into her resting-place. We took the child to safety and made our way back home to sleep. In the morning we had a job to do.

29 September, night – At twelve o'clock we went back to the tomb. We took off the coffin lid yet again. Lucy looked like a nightmare, a monster in the shape of a woman. Van Helsing took out his knives and some stakes about three feet long. They had been sharpened to a fine point. He had a heavy wooden hammer with him as well. When all was ready, the Professor spoke.

'This is one of the un-dead. Such creatures feed upon the living and turn them into vampires. If she had kissed you, Arthur, you too would be un-dead. If we let her live, those children would come to her and they would become vampires. But if we kill this devil,

77

the wounds on their throats will vanish. We must really kill this Lucy and send her soul to the angels.'

He turned to Arthur. 'You must help me.'

'Go on,' said Arthur. 'Tell me what I must do.'

'Take this stake in your left hand. Place the point over the heart and hold the hammer ready. When I read the prayer for the dead, you must strike. Strike in the name of God!'

Arthur picked up the hammer and stake and waited. He did not tremble. Van Helsing began to read. Arthur placed the point over the heart. As I looked I could see it make a mark in the white flesh. Then he struck it with all his strength.

The thing in the coffin twisted and turned like a snake. A horrible scream came from the open red lips. The body shook and twisted and the sharp white teeth bit together until the lips were cut. The mouth was smeared with a red foam. But Arthur did not weaken. He drove the stake deeper and deeper. The blood came out and spurted up from the heart.

And then the body stopped twisting. The teeth stopped biting together and the face stopped twitching. At last Lucy lay still. Our terrible job was over.

The hammer fell from Arthur's hand. He staggered and would have fallen if we had not caught him. Great drops of sweat appeared on his forehead. His breath came in broken gasps. It had been a great strain for him. We were so busy looking at him we did not look at the coffin. But when we did, we were filled with surprise. Arthur got up and looked into the coffin. His face became less horrified and he almost smiled.

The foul thing that we had so hated had gone. In the coffin lay the body of Lucy. She was her beautiful self again. Her face looked holy and calm. It was as if a storm had passed and given way to sunshine.

Arthur bent and kissed her. Then we sent him and Quincey out of the tomb. The Professor and I sawed the top off the stake. We left the point of it in the body. Then we cut off the head and filled the mouth with garlic.

Outside, the air was sweet. The sun shone, and the birds sang. There was joy and peace and laughter everywhere.

Before we moved away, Van Helsing said, 'Now, my friends. One step of our work is done. But there remains a greater task. We must find Count Dracula and destroy him. It will be a long and difficult search full of terrible danger. Will you help me?'

We each took his hand in turn and made a promise to help him destroy the evil of Dracula.

18 In the asylum

Dr Seward's diary

(*Note: Nobody knows yet that Dracula's coffin is in the place next to Dr Seward's lunatic asylum. Then Jonathan remembers. . . .*)

30 September – Van Helsing, Arthur and Quincey have gone to the British Museum in London. They are going to search that wonderful library for books on vampires.

I have just been introduced by Van Helsing to Jonathan and Mina Harker. I have read the amazing diary of the husband. He thinks that the Count may live in the house near this asylum! It is difficult to believe that the evil creature has been living on our doorstep all this time! Jonathan then felt rather ill so he went to bed. He wants to be fresh for meeting us all together tonight.

Later – I am just beginning to tie in the case of Renfield with the whole story of Count Dracula. I had the sudden idea of taking Mina Harker to meet the lunatic, and Mina agreed. She is a brave woman.

I went into Renfield's room first, and told him a lady would like to see him. His reply was, 'Oh, very well. Let her come in, but just let me tidy up the place.'

His method of tidying was really disgusting. He simply swallowed all the flies and spiders from the boxes, before I could stop him. When he had done this, he said, 'Let the lady come in.' Then he sat down on the edge of his bed.

Mina came in the room. I was worried that Renfield might plan an attack on her, so I stood by just in case. But Mina and Renfield chatted together like old friends. I was amazed. She must be a very kind woman for him to trust her like that! The lunatic explained that he had been mad for a long time. He has the idea that he can live for ever if he eats living things. He said that he had even tried to take a human life.

When we left, Renfield took the lady by both hands and said, 'You are in danger here. I hope I never see your sweet face again. May God bless and keep you!'

I think Renfield has even fallen in love with Mina Harker!

Mina Harker's diary

30 September – We all met in Dr Seward's study in the asylum at about eight o'clock this evening. Jonathan and I, Arthur, Quincey and Dr Seward sat round a table while Van Helsing spoke.

'I think it is good for you to know all about our enemy,' he said. 'I will tell you all I know.' He stopped and stared at some notes on his desk. 'There really are such beings as vampires. We all have proof of this. Except for Mrs Harker, we have all seen a vampire with our own two eyes. There is proof in books written by others as well. I used to think they were writing nonsense, but now I know they are true.'

Van Helsing stopped for a moment. He stared at each of us in turn. 'This creature has the strength of twenty men,' he went on. 'He is several hundred years old and has great cunning. He has the cruelty of the devil. He has power over the weather and can send storms, fog and thunder. He can make animals such as the rat, the owl, the bat, the moth, the fox and the wolf obey him. He can become large or small and can sometimes completely disappear.'

The old Professor stopped once more. We held our breath and waited. 'Then how can we destroy him?' he said. 'How can we find all his resting-places and destroy them too? That is what we must now do. We must be ready to face great danger. If we fail, we too may become vampires. We would end up feasting upon the bodies and souls of the people we love. The gates of heaven will never open for us if we become un-dead. We will become enemies of God and Christ. Are you willing to take such a risk?'

'Mina and I will take the risk,' said Jonathan.

As he spoke, Jonathan took my hand. I was frightened but his touch gave me comfort.

'Count me in,' said Quincey.

'And me,' added Dr Seward and Arthur.

Van Helsing took a deep breath and became more cheerful. 'Our enemy is strong,' he said, 'but we are also strong. We have modern science to help us and we can act both by day and by night.' He smiled at us, then looked down at his notes.

'Vampires have been known throughout history. They have been found in ancient Greece and Rome, in Germany, France, India and even in far-off China. The vampire does not die of old age. He can even grow younger if he finds enough victims. He never eats food and has no shadow. He has no reflection in a mirror. He can turn himself into a wolf or a bat. This man can make mist around himself. He can move through the moonlight and can look like coloured mist – just as those women did in Castle Dracula.'

The Professor stopped and smiled at us. 'Don't look so worried,' he said. 'In many ways the vampire is a slave. He cannot enter a house unless someone first asks him to come in. But then he can enter and leave as he pleases. He is the prisoner of the night. He never walks in daylight. He must return to his coffin at sunrise or die. He cannot cross running water. Some things can take away his power. These are garlic, and the cross. A wild rose put on his coffin will keep him trapped there. A holy bullet fired into his coffin will destroy him. A stake driven through his heart will kill him. He would also be truly dead if we cut off his head.'

He went on, 'A friend in Budapest tells me that this vampire must be one of the line of Counts Dracula, who won many battles against the Turks. If this is so, he is no ordinary vampire. The Draculas are a noble family of rulers, but they use black magic.'

As Van Helsing was talking, Quincey Morris noticed something at the window. He went over to look. He did this quietly, not wishing to disturb anyone. The Professor went on talking.

'This is what we must do. We have found out that coffins of earth were sent from Castle Dracula to Whitby. They were all delivered to the house nearby. I have also found out that some of the boxes were taken away and moved somewhere else. Clearly, the vampire wants to spread them out over the country. He wants to come and go where he pleases. We must get into the house and have a look. We must find all those coffins of earth and –'

Suddenly, we heard the sound of a pistol shot. The window was smashed by a bullet. The bullet hit the ceiling and struck the far wall. I shouted out in fear. Dr Seward rushed over to the window and threw up the sash. Then, we heard Quincey's voice outside.

'Sorry! I didn't mean to frighten you. I'll come in and tell you what happened.' A minute later he came in.

'It was a stupid thing to do,' he said. 'I must beg your pardon, Mrs Harker. I did not mean to scare you. But while the Professor was talking, I saw a huge bat on the window sill. I went outside to have a shot at it. It could have been Count Dracula!'

'Did you hit it?' said Van Helsing.

'I don't think so. I saw it fly away into a wood. That's strange, you know. Bats usually fly in circles but this one flew straight. It was as if it knew exactly where it was going.'

Quincey sat down and the Professor began to speak again.

'We must find all those coffins. When we are ready, we must capture or kill this monster. We must pour holy water in his coffins, or cover them all with pieces of holy bread. I say we should go to that house now and look at those boxes of earth.'

He turned to me and said, 'Mrs Harker, the men will do this alone. You can stay here and rest. We do not want to put your life in danger.'

They have now gone off to the house. It is difficult for me to sleep while my husband is in danger, but I must try.

Dr Seward's diary

1 October, 4 a.m. – Just as we were about to leave the asylum a message came from Renfield. He wanted to see me at once. I told the male nurse that it would have to wait until the morning. But the nurse said that Renfield would become violent if I did not see him. Van Helsing, Arthur, Quincey and Jonathan said it might be a good idea if we all saw him together. We went into the room, and Renfield made a short speech.

'I am now as sane as any of you. I wish to be let free tonight. I have not long to live and I want to enjoy life outside these prison walls.'

'That is out of the question,' I said.

'What do I have to say or do to prove that I am no longer mad?' he asked.

'If you behave yourself for the next few weeks, I may set you free,' I said.

'I must be set free tonight!' said Renfield.

'No!' I said. 'We must go now. We have work to do.' I expected Renfield to sulk or to become violent. But he went down on his knees, and begged me with tears in his eyes.

'Please, doctor, please! Let me out of this house at once. Send me away. Send me anywhere. Put me in chains and send me to a real prison, but let me out of this place. My soul is in danger. Don't you hear me? Can't you understand? Will you never learn? I am no longer a lunatic. I am well and I am fighting for my soul. Listen to me! Let me go! Let me go! Let me go!'

I did not want him to go into a fit, so I told him to go to his bed. Suddenly he stopped. He stared into my face for a while. Then he did as he was told.

As we were leaving, he said in a quiet voice, 'Dr Seward, I hope that later on you will remember what I have said.'

I was amazed by his behaviour once more.

And now I must stop writing. We are ready to visit the house nearby. We must track down this evil Count.

19 Attacked by rats

Jonathan Harker's diary

1 October – As we left the room, Quincey Morris turned to Dr Seward.

'Say, Jack, if that man wasn't trying to trick us, he is not a madman at all. I believe he really was worried about losing his soul. You seemed a bit hard on him.'

'I don't agree,' replied Dr Seward. 'That man is no ordinary lunatic. I cannot trust him. He seems to be mixed up with the Count. Also, he has a habit of eating spiders and flies. He also once tried to rip out my throat with his teeth. If the Count has power over wolves and rats, he may have power over madmen.'

'Talking of rats,' Arthur said, 'that old place may be full of them. But I've got something that will take care of the rats.' He held up a little silver whistle.

Soon, we were in the grounds of the Count's house. We kept in the shadows. We did not want to be taken in by some policeman as a gang of burglars. The Professor opened his bag. He took out four little bundles. He gave each of us a little silver cross and a wreath of garlic to wrap round our necks. Then he gave us a revolver and knife. We could use these to fight against animals and people in the Count's power. We were also given a small torch and an envelope which held some pieces of holy bread.

We lit our lamps and entered the ruined building. Huge shadows seemed to dance before us. We kept looking over our shoulders. The whole place was thick with dust and spiders' webs. At last we came to a wooden door with rusty hinges. We pulled it open. The smell was foul. It was the smell of blood and evil. There were the coffins, but we counted only twenty-nine out of fifty!

Suddenly I saw Arthur turn and look out of the door. He looked into the passage outside. I turned to look as well. I seemed to see the Count's evil face in the shadows. I thought I saw the ridge of his nose, the red eyes, the red lips, and the awful white skin. It was only for a moment, then it was gone.

Arthur said at the same moment, 'I thought I saw a face, but it must have been the shadows.' We went out into the passage but saw nothing.

A few minutes later, I saw Quincey step back suddenly. He had been looking in a corner. A cloud of coloured dust had risen up which twinkled with stars.

Then we became aware that the whole place was alive with rats. For a moment, we stood frozen with horror. But Arthur was ready for this. He rushed to the door and swung it open. He took his little silver whistle from his pocket. He blew a low, loud call.

Next we heard the yelping of dogs. A minute later, three small dogs came rushing in. There were about four times as many rats as before. They seemed to swarm all over the place. The lamplight shone on their dark bodies and shining eyes. The dogs stopped at the doorway. They began to howl in a most frightening way. Arthur picked one up, carried it into the room and dropped it on the floor. The moment its feet touched the ground it got back its courage and rushed upon the rats. The rats began to run away in terror. The other two dogs were also carried into the room. One minute later, the rats had completely vanished.

Van Helsing was pleased. 'The Count has power over the rats, but he cannot make them fight against other animals. Good. Perhaps he is less powerful than we thought. Let us now go home, because it will soon be dawn. We can be very pleased with this night's work.'

When we got back, the asylum was silent. But then we heard some poor madman screaming away in one of the far rooms. A low moaning sound came from Renfield's room. The poor fellow must have been having a nightmare.

I crept into our own room and found Mina asleep. She was breathing so softly I had to put my ear down to hear it. She looks paler than usual. I hope last night's meeting did not upset her too much. I rested on the sofa so as not to disturb her.

1 October, later – I suppose it was to be expected that we should oversleep. It was such a busy day and the night before I had no rest at all. Even Mina must have been very tired. She slept until this afternoon. I had to shout three times to make her wake. When she opened her eyes, there was a look of terror in them. It was as if she had come out of a bad dream.

We now know that twenty-one boxes have been taken away from the Count's house. They will all have to be found. We will meet later tonight to decide what to do.

20 Dracula strikes again

Mina Harker's diary

1 October – Last night I went to bed when the men had
gone, I tried to sleep, because they had told me to.
But I did not feel sleepy. I kept thinking about
Jonathan being trapped in Castle Dracula. I thought
about the death of poor Lucy. I began to cry and felt
ashamed. Jonathan must not see that I have been
weeping. . . .

I can't quite remember how I fell asleep in the end.
I remember hearing the sudden barking of the dogs
and a lot of queer sounds. I heard the sound of prayers.
They came from Mr Renfield's room. Then there was
silence. I could not hear a sound anywhere. This
worried me, so I got up. I looked out of the window.
Everything was dark and silent. The black shadows
made by the moonlight were very frightening. A thin
streak of mist was slowly creeping across the grass. It
came towards the house as if it had a life of its own.
Suddenly I felt very tired. It was as if I had been
drugged. I went back to bed, but I still could not
sleep.

Once again I got up and went to the window. Now
the mist was close to the house. It lay thick against the
wall. It seemed to creep up to the windows. Renfield's
moaning was getting louder all the time. Then there

was the sound of a struggle, and I knew that the male nurses were dealing with the lunatic. I was so frightened that I crept into bed. I pulled the clothes over my head and put my fingers in my ears. I still did not feel sleepy, but somehow or other I must have fallen asleep. I do not remember anything more except a bad dream. It was a very strange dream.

In my dream I seemed to be asleep. I was waiting for Jonathan to come back. I was very worried about him. I felt as though my arms and legs had weights on them. I remembered that the air had suddenly become damp and cold. I put back the clothes from my face and found that the mist had grown thicker. It had poured into the room. The gaslight seemed to glow like a tiny red spark in this fog. I wanted to close the window, but I felt as if I had been frozen. Then I noticed that the window was closed. The fog was pouring through the gaps in the door. It looked like smoke but it had the force of boiling water. It grew thicker and thicker. It became a kind of pillar of steam. I could see a light shining through it, like a red eye. Things began to spin in my brain. Suddenly a horrible thought came to me. It was like this when Jonathan had seen those vile women. In my dream I must have fainted. Everything went black. But I thought I saw a white face bending over me out of the mist.

I must be careful of such dreams. They might drive me mad. I will ask Dr Seward or Van Helsing for a sleeping drug if I have another dream like this. But I do not want to disturb them. They have enough on their minds as it is. They do not want to worry about a woman who might be going mad.

2 October, 10 p.m. – I slept last night, but I did not

dream. Today I feel very weak. I don't know why, as I spent the whole day lying down and dozing. Mr Renfield asked to see me in the afternoon. The poor man was very gentle. When I went away he kissed my hand, and he asked God to bless me. I find I cry whenever I think of him. I must not let Jonathan know. This is no time for me to have a breakdown.

Dr Seward gave me a sleeping pill for tonight, but I did not tell him about my dream. I now feel sleepy and a bit afraid. Perhaps I was foolish to take the drug. But it is too late now. Here comes sleep. Good night. . . .

21 An attack on Renfield

Dr Seward's diary

1 October – Van Helsing and Quincey are busy trying to find the missing coffins. We have found out that they were taken to various parts of London by three or four removal firms.

I am worried about Renfield. I am sure he has something to do with the Count. He has begun to catch spiders and flies again.

2 October – I must try to keep calm. Good God! After this evening, we seem to be living a terrible nightmare. Either that or we have all gone mad.

It all started with a wild yell from Renfield's room.

Moments later, the attendants came rushing into my room. They told me that Renfield had been hurt. When I got to his room, I found him lying on the floor. He lay in a shining pool of blood. His body looked broken and twisted. I turned him over and saw that his face was badly hurt. It looked as if it had been battered against the floor. In fact the pool of blood was spreading out from his face.

One of the male nurses said, 'I think his back is broken, sir. He cannot move his right arm and leg. The whole side of his face is smashed.'

The nurse scratched his head. 'I can't understand it,' he said. 'He might have hurt his face by beating his own head against the floor. He might have broken his neck by falling out of bed. But I can't see how he could do *both* at the same time.'

'Go to Van Helsing,' I said, 'and tell him to come at once.' The man ran off. A few minutes later, the Professor came. He was wearing his dressing-gown and slippers.

'Ah!' he said. 'A sad accident. I have brought my instruments.' He whispered to me. 'Send the nurse away. We must be alone with Renfield when he comes round.'

So I said to the nurse, 'I think that will do now, Simmons. We have done all we can for the moment. You had better go now. Dr Van Helsing will operate. Let me know if anything unusual happens anywheer else.'

The man left, and we looked at Renfield carefully. His face was not really so serious. But his skull had been badly broken. We would have to operate, or blood clots would form in the brain. Arthur and Quincey came in. They watched us in silence.

When we had finished, we waited for Renfield to open his eyes. The time seemed to pass very slowly. The poor man's breathing came in deep, sobbing gasps. At times he opened his eyes as if about to speak. But then he closed them again. I could hear my own heartbeats. The silence became terrible.

Suddenly the Professor spoke. 'There is no time to lose. We must get him to speak. It may save somebody's life. It may save his own soul. We will operate again, just above the ear.'

He started the second operation. Renfield's breathing continued to be heavy. Then he gasped and his eyes flew open. He stared at me and groaned.

'I'll be quiet, Doctor. Tell them to take off my strait-jacket. I have had a terrible dream. It has left me so weak I cannot move. What's wrong with my face? It feels cut, and it hurts.'

Van Helsing spoke. 'Tell us about your dream, Mr Renfield.'

'It was not a dream,' the man groaned. 'It was real. Quick, Doctor, give me some brandy. I must say everything before I die. I know my brain is crushed.'

Quincey Morris came rushing in. He had a flask, and we gave the man something to drink.

'Thank you. It began on the night I begged you to let me go. He came to the window. He had turned himself into a cloud of fog. I have seen him do that before. His eyes were fierce. His red mouth was laughing. His sharp white teeth shone in the moonlight. He wanted me to ask him to come in. At first I said no. Then he began to bribe me.'

Renfield was stopped by a word from the Professor. 'How?'

'He sent me huge flies when the sun was shining. He sent me big moths during the night. Then he promised to send me rats as well. I laughed and I asked him to prove he could do this. The dogs began to howl in the dark trees. I went to the window. I saw him lift up his hands. He seemed to call out without using any words. The mist disappeared. Then I could see thousands of rats with tiny red eyes. His voice spoke: "I will give you all these rats and many more, if you fall down and worship me!" I opened the window and said to him, "Come in, Lord and Master!"'

Renfield's voice had grown weaker. I poured some more brandy into his mouth. He went on,

'The next day I waited, but he sent me nothing. When he came during the night, I was angry. But he just laughed. He acted as if he owned the place, and I was nothing. Then somehow I felt that Mrs Harker had come into the room.'

Quincey and Arthur came over. They wanted to listen more carefully. The Professor gave a gasp. I began to feel very worried. Renfield went on. He did not notice our alarm.

'When Mrs Harker came to see me this afternoon she wasn't the same. She was pale. I knew that he had been taking the life out of her. I was angry. The next time he came I grabbed him with my madman's strength. But his red eyes turned my strength to water. He lifted me up and flung me down. I heard my head beat the floor in a noise like thunder. Then the mist began to creep under the door.'

Renfield's voice was very weak now. His eyes looked like glass. We knew he would soon die. Van Helsing stood up.

'We must be armed against the Count. Get the

things you had last night. Quick. There is not a moment to spare.'

We stopped outside Mina's door. Van Helsing turned the handle, but it was locked. We all threw ourselves against the wood. It burst open with a crash. We went tumbling into the room. I picked myself up. What I saw made me gasp with horror. I felt my hair stand up on the back of my neck. My heart seemed to stop.

22 The curse of Dracula

Dr Seward's diary (continued)

2 October, still – The moonlight was pouring into the room. Jonathan Harker lay on the bed by the window. His face was red. He was breathing heavily as though drugged. His wife was kneeling on the edge of the bed. She was dressed in white.

A tall thin man dressed in black was standing by her. His face was turned away from us at first. But when he spun round, we all saw it was the Count. He had been holding Mina Harker by the neck and was forcing her to drink the blood that trickled from his own chest. It was like some child forcing a kitten's nose into milk to make it drink.

As the Count turned to face us, we saw his eyes were red. He trembled with rage. The white sharp teeth bit hard together like those of a wild beast. He threw Mina to one side and turned to face us with his red lips dripping blood. Then he sprang towards us. I thought the end had come.

But the Professor got to his feet. He held out the envelope which contained the holy bread. The Count stopped. He moved back as if afraid. We went towards him holding up our crosses. Suddenly a great black cloud sailed across the moon. The room went completely black. We could not see a thing. Quincey switched on his torch. We saw nothing at first. Then we saw a faint mist which sank under the door and disappeared. The Count had escaped!

Suddenly Mina Harker took a deep breath. She gave a wild scream. It was so terrible I think it will ring in my ears till my dying day. Her face was like that of a ghost. Her lips, cheek and chin were smeared with blood. A thin stream trickled from her throat and her eyes were mad with terror.

Van Helsing whispered to me, 'Jonathan has been hypnotized and drugged by the vampire. We must leave poor Mina until she calms down. I shall wake Jonathan.'

He dipped the end of a towel in cold water and began to flick Jonathan's face with it. Mina held her face in her hands and wept.

I lifted the blind and looked out of the window. In the moonlight I saw Quincey Morris. He ran across the lawn and hid himself in the shadow of a large tree. This puzzled me, but before I could see any more I heard Jonathan awake. For a few moments he lay still. Then he jumped up in alarm. His wife turned to him. She held out her arms as if to hold him. Then she stopped and shivered till the bed shook beneath her.

'In God's name, what does this mean?' Jonathan cried out. 'What has happened? What is wrong? Mina? What does this blood mean? My God! God help her! Has it come to this?' He turned to Van Helsing: 'Help her, please help her! It cannot have gone very far yet. Look after her while I go to look for that creature.'

His wife suddenly grabbed hold of him and cried out, 'No, Jonathan! You must not leave me. I have gone through enough tonight. You must stay with me!'

Van Helsing tried to calm her, but she caught sight of the blood on her nightdress. She felt the cuts on her neck. She let out a cry.

'I am evil, evil. I am dirty. I must not touch or kiss my husband any more. I am the worst enemy of the man I love.'

'Nonsense!' cried Jonathan. 'I will not hear you say such things, Mina. Nothing will come between us. You stood by me in my time of madness, and I will stand by you.'

I told Jonathan what had happened in Renfield's room while he had been drugged by the vampire. Just as I finished, Arthur and Quincey ran into the Harkers' room. They had not found Dracula, but Quincey had something else to tell us.

'When the Count escaped in his mist, I hid outside in the shadow of a tree and waited. I did not see the Count, but I did see a bat come out from Renfield's window. It flapped towards the west. I expected it to go back to the house. But he seems to have gone somewhere else. He will not be back tonight. The sky is now red in the east. It will soon be light. We have work to do tomorrow!'

Van Helsing put his hand gently on Mina's head.

'And now, Mina, you must help us. We need to know all we can. Could you please tell us exactly what happened?'

The poor, dear girl shivered. She held her husband's hand and began.

'I took the sleeping drug I had been given, but I could not sleep. I began to think of death and vampires. I thought of blood, pain and trouble. But at last I went to sleep. I did not wake up when Jonathan came to bed. Much later, I did wake up and saw my husband fast asleep. A thin white mist was in the room, and I was afraid. I tried to wake Jonathan, but he slept as if he had been drugged. I looked around in terror. There stood a tall thin man, all in black. I knew him at once from all I have heard. His eyes were red. There was also a red scar on his forehead. This must be where Jonathan once hit him with a shovel. I wanted to scream but I was somehow frozen. The man then spoke in a sharp whisper.

' "Silence!" he said. "If you make a sound I shall smash the brains out of your husband before your very eyes." With an evil smile, he placed one hand upon my shoulder. He held me tight, and began to stroke my throat. "First I must have something to drink. I am thirsty. You may as well let me. *I have already drunk your blood twice before.*" I did not try to stop him. I suppose it is part of the curse. I felt as if I had been hypnotized. And then, God save me! He placed his evil lips upon my throat. I fainted. When I woke, his lips were covered with fresh blood. Then he spoke in his evil way. "You little fool! Did you think you could defeat me? You will be my slave. I will drink your blood like wine. Then you will become one of us.

You will obey my orders wherever you are. Even if I am hundreds of miles away, we will still be together, you and I. Your blood and mine will be the same!' He undid his shirt. With one of his long sharp nails he cut open a vein in his chest. When the blood began to spurt out, he forced my mouth to the wound. I was forced to swallow some of his . . . Oh my God! my God! what have I done? God pity me!'

Then Mina began to rub her lips as if to make them clean.

As she told the terrible story, the dawn broke. We were all silent. A dreadful curse has come upon us.

23 The coffins

Jonathan Harker's diary

3 October – Renfield is now dead. He will be buried as soon as possible. Van Helsing and Dr Seward have managed to trace some missing coffins to a house in Piccadilly. We all met during the afternoon to make plans for the future. We hoped we would be able to find all the Count's coffins and destroy them. Poor Mina said she would kill herself if she began to turn into a vampire. I made her promise never to take her own life whatever happened. Before we set off for the house in Piccadilly, Van Helsing spoke to us.

'Now, my dear friends, we will set out for our

enemy's hiding place. But first I must help Mina to fight against the evil of the vampire.' He turned towards her. 'On your forehead I touch this piece of holy bread, in the name of the Father, the Son and –'

There was a fearful scream. It almost froze our hearts. The holy bread had burned the flesh like a piece of white-hot metal. Mina sank to her knees on the floor. She was in agony. She pulled her beautiful hair over her face and cried out.

'I am evil! I am filthy! Even God hates me now! I must wear this mark of shame upon my forehead until the day I die.'

I took Mina in my arms and held her tight. In my heart I made a promise. If Mina turned into a vampire, I would join her, and God have mercy on both our souls.

Dr Seward's diary

3 October – Van Helsing, Arthur, Quincey, Jonathan and myself made our way to the house in Piccadilly. We broke in, and found several coffins in one of the rooms. We smashed them all to pieces, except one. We waited round this one evil-smelling box to catch the Count when he came back to it. I kept looking at Jonathan, and I felt great pity for him. The poor fellow had gone grey overnight. Yesterday, he was brown-haired and full of life. Now his eyes are hollow and his forehead is lined with sorrow. We waited and the seconds seemed to pass with the slowness of a nightmare. Then slow, careful steps came along the hall.

Suddenly the Count leaped into the room. Jonathan threw himself in front of the door to stop him getting out again. A horrible growl came from the Count's throat. We moved forward together and Harker stabbed at him with his great knife. It was a powerful cut and only the Count's quickness saved him. Had he been slower, the blade would have cut through his heart. As it was, the knife cut through his coat and made a wide hole. A bundle of bank notes and a stream of gold fell out. The Count's hand reached for Jonathan's throat. His mouth was opened to bite. Then I moved forward holding a cross. A great power seemed to fly along my arm, and I saw the monster move back in fear. The Count's face was filled with hate and rage. It had become yellow, and the red scar on his forehead burned like a flame. The Count dived underneath Jonathan's arm. He grabbed a handful of money from the floor. Then he dashed across the room, and threw himself at the window. The glass smashed into pieces.

The Count fell on to the paving stones below. I could hear the clink of the gold. Some of the coins had dropped out of his hand.

We ran over and saw him jump again. He was not hurt. He rushed up some steps and pushed open a stable door. There he turned to face us.

'You cannot defeat me! You are like sheep in a butcher's shop, waiting to be killed. You will be sorry, all of you! My revenge has just begun. I have already taken your women. I have made them my creatures. Filth!'

With an evil laugh, he disappeared through the door. It was useless to follow him. We stood and watched his black shape disappear behind a wall. Then we broke up this coffin as well.

Van Helsing was the first to speak. 'We have learned

a great deal. He is afraid of us. Did you notice it in his voice? Did you see the way he grabbed for the money? He does not know which way to turn. We have destroyed almost all of his coffins. Our enemy is near to defeat!'

24 Hypnotism

Jonathan Harker's diary

3–4 October, close to midnight – We were fools to think the Count was near to defeat. We know that one more coffin is left if the Count is still alive, but only the Count knows where it is. Our enemy may escape us for years. All we can do is sit and wait. Poor Mina! What will become of her, and what will become of me? *Later* – I must have fallen asleep. I was woken up by Mina. She was sitting up in bed. There was a surprised look on her face. She had placed a warning hand over my mouth. She whispered in my ear, 'Hush! There is someone in the corridor!'

I got up softly. I crossed the room and gently opened the door. Just outside lay Quincey. He was lying on a mattress. He was wide awake.

'Go back to bed,' he said. 'It is all right. One of us will be here all night. We don't mean to take any chances!'

I came back and told Mina. She sighed and almost managed to smile. She put her arms round me and said softly, 'Oh thank God for good brave men!' With a sigh she went back to sleep again.

4 October, morning – Once again during the night I was woken up by Mina. The day was just beginning to break. 'Quick!' she gasped. 'Go and call the Professor. I want to see him at once.'

'Why?' I asked.

'I have an idea. Quick! The Professor must hypnotize me before the sun rises. Go quick!' I went to the door. Dr Seward was resting on the mattress. When he saw me, he jumped to his feet.

'Is anything wrong?' he asked.

'No,' I replied, 'but Mina wants to see Dr Van Helsing at once.'

'I will go,' he said. He hurried into the Professor's room.

Two minutes later the Professor came in with Dr Seward, Arthur and Quincey.

'What can I do for you?' asked Van Helsing. He was smiling.

'I want you to hynotize me!' said Mina. 'Do it before the sun rises, for I feel I can only speak freely before the dawn. Be quick, for time is short!'

Van Helsing made her sit up in bed. He looked deep into her eyes. He moved first one hand and then the other above her forehead. Mina stared at him and my heart began to beat like a hammer. I felt something was going to happen. Her eyes slowly closed. She sat as still as a stone. The Professor moved his hands once more. Then he stopped. I could see his forehead was covered with great drops of sweat. Mina opened her eyes, but she did not seem the same woman. There was a faraway look in her eyes. Her voice sounded strange, sad and dreamy. Van Helsing spoke in a low voice. He did not want to disturb her thoughts.

'Where are you?'

'I do not know. I am asleep,' Mina said. There was silence for a while. Mina sat still and the Professor stared at her. The rest of us hardly dared to breathe. The room was growing lighter. Van Helsing told me to lift the blind. Mina was covered in the light of the early morning.

The Professor spoke again. 'Where are you now?'

She answered dreamily, and seemed to be speaking the thoughts of another person. 'I do not know. It is all strange to me!'

'What do you see?' asked the Professor.

'I can see nothing. It is all dark,' Mina said.

'What do you hear?'

'The sound of water. There are waves. I can hear them outside,' Mina said.

'Then you are on a ship?' We all looked at each other. We were excited. The answer came quickly.

'Oh yes!'

'What else do you hear?' The Professor asked.

'The sound of men stamping overhead. They are running about. There is the creaking of a chain.'

'What are you doing?' asked the Professor.

'I'm still – oh, so still. It is like death!' Mina's voice got softer and softer. Her open eyes closed again. She was asleep.

'What does it mean?' I asked.

Van Helsing looked at me and smiled. 'The blood of Dracula is in her veins. She is able to read his thoughts even though he is many miles away.'

'Then the vampire is on board a ship. Is it a ship somewhere in London?' I asked.

'Correct,' the Professor said.

'Let's go then! Quick!' I said.

The Professor lifted his hand. 'Not so fast, my friend.' He laughed. 'That ship was taking up its anchor. There are many ships getting ready to leave London at this time. You do not know which one to look for. But let us thank God that we have a clue at last. We have been blind, but now we can see. When the Count grabbed at that money he was afraid. He wanted to escape. Think about it – ESCAPE. He knew that he had only one coffin left. He knew that he would be chased like a fox running from a pack of dogs. He knew London was no place for him. That is why he took his last coffin on board a ship.'

Mina suddenly broke in. She had woken up. She had heard every word of the Professor.

'But why do we need to follow him? He has gone for good. He will not come back.'

Van Helsing looked at her sadly. 'We must follow him into the jaws of hell. He can live for hundreds of years. We have a duty to save the world from this evil creature. We must find him quickly. There is no time to lose. Remember, he has put that mark upon your throat.'

I was just in time to catch Mina as she fell forward. She had fainted. I put her on the bed and gritted my teeth. Dracula must be destroyed. For the sake of the world and for the sake of the woman I love. At least now we have a chance.

25 The chase to Varna

Mina Harker's diary

5 October 5 p.m. – Van Helsing tells me that Dracula
is trying to go back to Transylvania. He says that only
one ship is going anywhere in that direction. This is
the *Princess Catherine*. It is a sailing ship. Quincey and
the Professor went to an office by the docks. They
learned that a tall thin man with white teeth and
red-looking eyes had been to the office. This man
had given the captain gold to take a large box on
board.

The thin man had come on board to see the box put
in a safe place. Then a mist had covered the ship. The
thin man had disappeared. Soon after, the ship had
set sail. Van Helsing hoped to catch up with the box
at a placed called Varna. I wish we could forget all
about the Count. But Van Helsing says he is too
dangerous to leave alone. He is a devil that must be
destroyed.

Ten minutes ago, I saw myself in the mirror. The
red mark is still upon my throat. I am still evil!

Dr Seward's diary

5 October – Van Helsing asked to see me today. He
said, 'Our poor dear Mina is changing.'

A cold shiver ran through me. My worst fears were true. Van Helsing went on.

'We must remember what happened to Lucy Westen. We must be careful. I can see Mina's face slowly changing into that of a vampire. It is only very slight, but I have noticed it. Her teeth are a little sharper. Her eyes are harder. I am also worried about hypnotizing her. The Count hypnotized her first. Suppose he makes her tell him all our plans?'

I nodded to show that I understood what he was trying to say. He continued.

'We must not tell her of our plans. It is for her own good.'

Later – We have learned that the *Princess Catherine* is on its way to Varna. We hope to get ourselves there twenty-four hours before the ship arrives. We have decided to take Mina with us. She may lead us to the Count if he manages to escape. She herself has begged us not to tell her our plans. She is so sensible, and we feel we can trust her. But we must always be on our guard.

11 October, evening – Mina asked to see all of us this evening.

'In the morning,' she said, 'we will set out on our task. Only God knows what dangers we are to face. You must remember that I am not the same as you. There is poison in my blood. It will destroy me.'

She looked at us all and there were tears in her eyes. She went on. 'If I turn into a vampire, you must drive a stake through my heart. You must cut off my head. I am not afraid of death, but I do not want to lose my soul. I do not want to become an evil creature of the night.'

Everyone agreed except Jonathan. 'Must I make such a promise?' he said.

'You must,' she said. 'It is your duty.'

The poor man agreed. We saw his grey head bend low with sadness.

Jonathan Harker's diary

15 October, Varna – We left Charing Cross on the twelfth. We got to Paris the same night. Then we travelled night and day by train to arrive here at Varna.. Now we are waiting for the *Princess Catherine* to come into port. Thank God Mina is well and getting stronger! Van Helsing hypnotized her again. He asked her what she could see and hear.

Her answer was, 'I can see nothing. All is dark. I can hear waves lapping against the ship. The water is rushing by. Sails are being blown by the wind. Masts and ropes are creaking. The wind is high. The ship is travelling fast. The *Princess Catherine* is still at sea. She is heading towards Varna.'

We have had dinner and are going to bed early. Tomorrow we will get on board the ship as soon as it arrives. Van Helsing wants us to board it during daylight. When we get to the Count we will deal with him as we did with poor Lucy – with a stake.

17 October – Everything is ready but the boat is one day late. If the Count is in the coffin, Van Helsing and Seward will cut off his head at once. They will drive a stake through his heart. The Professor says if we do this quickly, the Count's body will soon turn into dust. Then there would be no chance of us being held for murder or for cutting up a dead body.

24 October – We have waited a whole week. The ship has not arrived. What has gone wrong?

28 October – Van Helsing has just got a message. It says

that the *Princess Catherine* has put in at a place called Galatz. This place is many miles from Varna. The Count has escaped us!

26 The Count escapes again

Dr Seward's diary

28 October – The next train to Galatz is at 6.30 tomorrow. Van Helsing asked to see me alone today.

'I believe the Count knows we are here,' he said. 'He has read the mind of our young Mina. Now he wants to escape. He will try to stop Mina getting into his mind. We shall see if he succeeds. I will pray to God and try to send her mind to him. We shall see who is the stronger.'

29 October – This is written in the train from Varna to Galatz. Last night Mina was hypnotized again. It took far longer than usual. Van Helsing had to keep asking his questions again and again. At last her answer came.

'I can see nothing. There are no waves, but there is water running against the side of the boat. I can hear men's voices. There is the sound of a rowing boat. A gun is being fired somewhere. There is tramping of feet above my head. Chains are dragging along. What is this? There is a gleam of light. I can feel the air blowing upon me.'

Suddenly she sat up. She opened her eyes and said, 'Would none of you like a cup of tea? You must all be so tired.'

When she had gone, Van Helsing said, 'You see, my friends. The Count is close to land. However, he cannot get on shore unless the ship touches land or somebody carries him there. He cannot cross running water by himself.'

30 October – We waited until this morning. We held our breath as the Professor tried to hypnotize Mina once more. It was terribly difficult. We knew that this might be our last chance. When she spoke, her words sounded slow and strange.

'Something is going on. I can hear the sounds of men shouting. I can hear the howling of wolves. There is another sound, a strange one like –' She stopped. She became very white.

'Go on! Speak, I command you!' said Van Helsing in a loud voice. But there was despair in his eyes. The sun had risen. The red light was pouring through the windows of the train. Mrs Harker opened her eyes.

'Oh Professor,' she said, 'why are you shouting?'

As she said this, we heard the whistle of the train. We are near to Galatz. Everyone is very excited.

Jonathan Harker's diary

30 October – We arrived in Galatz today. We got on board the *Princess Catherine* at once. We met the captain who told us of his voyage. He said he had never had such a fast trip.

'Man!' he said, 'it was as if the devil had blown

wind into our sails. But when we g   near Galatz, some of the sailors asked me to throw overboard a big box which a queer-looking old man had given me just before we left London. They kept making the sign of the cross. Some of them dragged the box on deck. I had to hit one across the back with an iron bar to stop them throwing it into the water. After all, I had agreed to carry it on board. Soon after, a man came aboard with an order to take the box. His papers were all right, so I let him take the box. I was glad to get rid of the damn thing!'

We got the name and address of the man who had taken the box. We went to his house, but we could not find him anywhere. One of his neighbours said he had vanished two days ago. We went to the police station and asked about the man. We found out that his body had been found dead inside a churchyard. They said his throat had been torn open as if by some wild animal.

That was that. We have come to a stop. We went back to the hotel, where Mina was waiting for me. Must I . . . will I have to kill her?

Mina Harker's Diary

30 October, evening – The men were very tired when they came back. I told them all to lie down and rest. Jonathan is worn out. His face is lined with pain. I wonder what he is thinking.

I let them sleep for a while. Then I woke them up. 'Don't look so miserable,' I said. 'I have been thinking and looking at some maps. I think I know how to catch the Count.' The men sat up and I began to explain.

'The Count wants to return to his castle. He wants to get earth for more coffins. We must try to catch him there. That will be easier than you think. He will not travel by road, because it is too dangerous. People are curious. There will be customs officers to go through all the luggage. He will not travel by rail either. Trains are too often late, and he would fear being caught by his enemies. So the safest way for him is to travel by water. I have checked the map. There is only one river that goes near Castle Dracula. Jonathan has told us the Count was first brought from the castle by the gypsies. So we can expect them to help the Count again.'

When I had finished, Jonathan took me in his arms. He kissed me. The others kept shaking my hands. Dr Van Helsing said, 'Well done!' Mina is our teacher. Her eyes have seen where we were blind. Now we are on the right track again. We must carry guns. We may have to fight with those gypsies.'

'I have brought Winchester rifles,' said Quincey. 'They will also take care of the wolves.'

'Good!' said Van Helsing. 'And you will help him, Jonathan. So will Arthur. Do not be afraid for Mina. I will look after her. When we get nearer, Mina's hypnotic power may help us.'

Jonathan broke in angrily. 'You are not going to take Mina to that castle! She is ill. She is cursed by that devil. I will not let you take her into a death trap. Not for the world! Not for heaven or hell!' For a moment he was so angry he could not speak. Then he went on.

'Do you know what that place is? Have you seen that evil den? The moonlight is alive with ghostly shapes. Every speck of dust could be a terrible monster. Have you felt the vampire's lips on your throat?'

He turned to me and pointed to my forehead. He threw up his arms with a cry. 'Oh my God, what have we done to deserve this horror?' Then he sank down on a sofa. He looked near to breakdown.

Van Helsing sighed. He spoke in a very calm voice. 'Mina must come with us. If the Count escapes us, he may choose to sleep for a hundred years. Then he would call his vampires to him and Mina would be one of them. Can't you still hear their evil laugh?'

'All right,' said Jonathan. He gave a sob that shook his body. 'We are now in the hands of God!'

What is to become of me? I must put my hopes in the Professor. I will soon know what is to be be my fate. May God look after us all!

27 The two parties

Mina Harker's diary.

31 October – Dr Seward, Quincey and Arthur have gone up the river in a motor launch. Van Helsing and myself are going towards Castle Dracula by coach. The countryside is lovely and most interesting. But the people are very, very worried about witches and demons. We stopped at an inn, and when a serving woman saw the scar on my forehead she crossed herself. She put out two fingers to ward off the evil eye. They even put extra garlic in our food!

The Professor keeps hypnotizing me. He tells me I keep talking of creaking wood and lapping water. So our enemy is still on the river.

Dr Seward's diary

4 November – Our boat had an accident as it tried to force its way up the river. We have overtaken several other boats, but none was the Count's. Arthur managed to repair our boat. But I fear we have lost a lot of time. I am worried about Van Helsing and Mina. They will now arrive at Castle Dracula before we have time to get there. They will be in great danger.

Note written by Van Helsing

4 November – I write this to my old friend Jack Seward in case I do not see him again. It is now morning. I am writing beside a fire which I have kept burning all through the night. Mina has helped me. It is cold and the grey sky is full of snow.

Mina told me to follow a certain road, and I did so. We tried to sleep in the coach last night. We had furs to keep us warm. But Mina lay awake most of the time. She stared at me with eyes that seemed far too bright. When she slept, she looked almost too healthy. Her cheeks were very red. I was afraid for her.

I feel safe now, but I wonder what will happen when night comes.

5 November – When you read this, Jack, you will think I am mad. You will think that my brain has been destroyed by too much horror.

We travelled all yesterday. We kept getting nearer to the mountains. We came to a rough pathway just as it was getting dark. There on the top of a steep hill I saw the castle Jonathan had written about. It was none other than Castle Dracula!

The night fell suddenly. I became very afraid. I woke Mina and lit a fire. Then I drew a large ring round the two of us. Over this ring I passed some of the holy bread. All the time, Mina sat inside the ring. She was as still as a dead body. She grew whiter and whiter till she became like the snow. I asked her to step near the fire, which was outside the circle. She got up but came to a stop on the edge of the circle. I sighed with relief. If she could not escape, then the vampires could not enter!

Soon the horses began to scream. They tore at their harness until I went to comfort them. When they felt my hands they were quiet. It became colder and the fire began to die. I was about to step forward to throw on more wood when I stopped. The snow was flying in big circles, and there was a cold kind of mist. Even in the dark, there was a light made by the snow. It seemed to me that the snow and the mist began to look like women in long clothes. The silence was grim and dead. The horses trembled with terror. I rushed back into the circle. It was like a nightmare. I kept thinking of Jonathan's terrible experiences, and I seemed to catch sight of those vile women who tried to kiss him. The horses moaned in terror. I looked at Mina. She smiled at me. She looked so calm I picked up some wood and was about to leave the circle to put it on the fire. But she grabbed me and pulled me back.

Her voice was a low whisper. 'No! No! Do not leave the circle. You are safe here!'

I turned to her. I looked into her eyes and said, 'I am not frightened for myself. I am afraid of what might happen to you.' This made her laugh. It was a strange ghostly sound.

'Afraid for me! Why? I am safe from them, very safe.' For a moment I wondered what she meant. Then a puff of wind made the flame leap up. I could see the red scar on her forehead. Then, alas, I knew.

The figures of mist and snow came closer, but still kept outside the holy circle. Suddenly I saw them. They were the three women who had tried to kiss Jonathan's throat. I could see the swaying bodies, the bright hard eyes, the white teeth, the soft red lips. They kept smiling at poor dear Mina. Their laugh came through the silence of the night. They pointed to her and spoke. Their voices were sweet and horrible.

'Come, sister. Come to us. Come! Come!' I was terrified and turned to look at Mina. Her eyes were filled with fear and horror. I was glad. This proved that she was not one of them yet. I grabbed some of the holy bread and went towards them in order to put some wood on the fire. They moved back and I heard them laugh their low, horrid laugh. I was not afraid now. They could not attack me, and they could not enter the circle to get at Mina. The horses had stopped moaning. They lay still on the ground. The snow covered them and I knew that their terrors and sufferings had ended. They were dead.

We stayed inside the holy circle until the red light of dawn began to shine through the snow. The horrid figures disappeared. They moved away towards the castle.

At last the sun rose. I saw that Mina was fast asleep. The horses are all dead. I must have breakfast and then set about my terrible work. Thank God Mina is so calm in her sleep. I will be able to leave her safely in the holy circle.

Dr Seward's diary

5 November – When dawn came this morning, we saw the gypsies. They were driving away from the river with a kind of wagon. They looked as if they were protecting it with their lives. The snow is falling now and there is a strange excitement in the air. I can hear the howling of wolves. There is danger all round us. We must leave the boat now, and I have been able to buy some horses. The horses are nearly ready and we will be on our way soon. Sooner or later, someone or something is going to die, because of all this.

Van Helsing's memorandum

5 November, afternoon – I am not mad yet. Thank God for that!

When I left Mina inside the holy circle, I made my way to the castle. The doors were all open but I smashed them off their hinges. I did not want them to close on me and trap me. I knew where the chapel was to be found, thanks to Jonathan's diary. The air was heavy and breathing became difficult. At times I almost became dizzy. I could hear the far-off howling of wolves. This made me think of poor Mina. Should I go back to make sure she was safe, or kill the evil creatures in this castle? Mina was safe from vampires in the holy circle, but the wolves might tear her to pieces. In the end I decided it was slightly better for her to be eaten by wolves than to rest in the grave of a vampire.

I knew there were three graves to be found. I searched and searched until I found one of them. There was the body on top. Her hair was dark. She looked very beautiful and full of life. I shivered at the thought of murdering her. Perhaps others before me had lost their nerve. Perhaps they had waited and been hypnotized by such beauty. The sun would set and the woman would kiss him. And there would be one more vampire!

I felt myself being hypnotized. Her tomb was heavy and filled with the dust of hundreds of years. A horrid smell clung to the place. I was beginning to feel sleepy. I was almost asleep when a long, low cry came through the air. It was a cry so full of misery it awoke me at once. It was the voice of poor Mina that I heard.

I took a deep breath and began tearing away more coffin lids. I found another sister who was also dark and beautiful. Then I found the one with fair hair who had tried to kiss Jonathan. She was so full of beauty that my head began to whirl. I felt myself becoming hypnotized again. But God be thanked, the wail of Mina was still ringing in my ears. I found the courage to carry on. Nearby I found a huge, empty tomb on which was written one word:

DRACULA

This then was the un-dead home of the King of the Vampires! I put some of the holy bread on the tomb so that the Count could never return there again.

Then began my terrible task, and I hated it. I had to kill not one body but three! I remembered the evil of the vampires, and I remembered the look of peace on poor Lucy's face when we killed her. If I had not remembered this, I could not have gone on. I could not have done that butcher's work. I could not have faced the horrid screeching as the stake went in. I could not have faced the shaking and the twisting of their bodies. I would have run away in terror and left my work undone. But it is over now! For a short moment each one gave a smile as she died. Then they began to crumble into dust before my eyes.

Finally, I covered the entrances of the castle with garlic and bread so that the Count can never return there as a vampire.

I went back to the circle where Mina slept and stepped into it. She woke from her sleep and cried out. 'Come!' she said. 'Come away from this evil place! Let us go and meet Jonathan. I know he is coming towards us.' She looked pale and ill but I did not mind this. I would rather not remember the fresh red cheeks of those sleeping vampires.

And so we go to meet our friends – and Count Dracula.

28 The end of Dracula

Mina Harker's diary

6 November – It was late yesterday afternoon when we walked towards the east. We moved slowly. We were loaded down with furs and rugs to protect us from the cold and snow. When we had gone a mile, I became tired and sat down. Behind us, we could see the outline of Castle Dracula and the tops of the mountains.

Even now there was something evil about the place. Then we heard wolves howling. They were far off, but the sound filled us with terror. The Professor found a hollow in the rock, a place where we could fight off an attack. He cooked some food but I could not eat. Then he took his field-glasses from their case. He stood on top of the rock and began to search the horizon.

Suddenly he called out. 'Look! Mina, look! Look!' I jumped up and stood beside him on the rock. He handed me the field-glasses and pointed. The snow was falling more heavily. It swirled about in front of our eyes. But it was still possible to see a great distance. There was the river. It looked like a black ribbon in the snow. Nearer to us, I could see a group of men on horses. They were racing along. They were gathered round a long wagon which kept moving from side to side like a dog's tail wagging. I could see that they were gypsies of some kind.

On the cart was a great wooden box. My heart leaped as I saw it. I knew that the Count was lurking near. The evening was now drawing close. At sunset the Thing inside the box would escape. I turned to the Professor. But he had disappeared.

A moment later, I saw him below me. He drew a holy circle round the rock and shouted, 'At least you will be safe from him here!' He took the glasses from me. He waited for a whirl of snow to pass by. 'See,' he said, 'they are flogging the horses. They are going as fast as they can.'

He stopped and said in a sad, despairing voice, 'They are racing for the sunset. We may be too late. God's will be done!'

More snow came down. When it passed, he gave

another cry. 'Look! Look! Look! Two horsemen are following. They are coming up from the south. It must be Quincey and Jack. Take the glasses. Look before the snow blots it all out.' I took them and looked. I saw the two quite clearly. At the same time I saw two other men coming from the north, riding at full speed. I knew one of them was Jonathan. The other was Arthur. They, too, were chasing the cart. When I told the Professor, he shouted like a schoolboy. He got his rifle ready. I was given a revolver for, as we were speaking, the howling of the wolves came louder and closer. I could see here and there dots moving singly and in twos and threes and larger numbers. The wolves were coming together for their feast!

Every second seemed like a year. The wind came now in cruel bursts. The gypsies and the wagon came closer and closer. The Professor and I got down behind our rock. We had our weapons ready. We had made up our minds they should not pass.

All at once, two voices shouted 'Halt!' It was Quincey and Jonathan! The gypsies did not understand the language, but they knew what was wanted. They stopped the horses. As they did so, Dr Seward and Arthur leaped forward. The gypsies took out their knives and waited. Jonathan ignored the flashing knives in front of him and the howling of the wolves behind. He rushed through the circle of gypsies and jumped on to the cart. He threw the great box to the ground. Quincey had also burst through the circle of gypsies. He was clutching at his side and blood was spurting through his fingers. All the same he attacked one end of the box and, with the help of Jonathan, he ripped up the lid. The nails made a screeching sound. The top of the lid was thrown back.

By this time the gypsies had seen that the guns of Arthur, Dr Seward, the Professor and myself were all around them. They gave up the fight. The sun was almost down behind the mountain tops. The shadows of the whole group fell upon the snow. I saw the Count lying inside the box. There was earth on his chest. He was as pale as death. He looked just like a wax doll. His red eyes glared with a horrible cruel look.

Those eyes saw the sinking sun and the look of hate turned to evil joy.

But, at that moment, Jonathan's great knife came down. I saw it cut through the throat. At the same moment, Quincey's knife plunged into the heart.

It was like a miracle. Before our very eyes, the whole body crumbled into dust and disappeared.

Even in the moment of his final death a look of peace came to the Count's face. It is something I shall never forget as long as I live.

The Castle of Dracula could be seen against the red sky. Every stone of its broken walls was lit by the rays of the setting sun.

The gypsies turned without a word. They rode away as if for their lives. The wolves followed them. We were left alone.

Quincey suddenly fell to the ground. He held his hand to his side. Blood poured through his fingers. I ran to him. The holy circle did not keep me back any more. Jonathan knelt behind him. Quincey put his head back on Jonathan's shoulder, took my hand and sighed, 'I am only too happy to have been of service! Oh God!'

He cried out suddenly, struggling up into a sitting position. He pointed to my forehead. 'It was worth dying for this! Look! Look!'

The sun was now right on the edge of the mountain top. The red light fell full upon my face. The men all went down on their knees. A deep 'Amen' came from their mouths.

The dying man spoke: 'God be thanked. Look! Her forehead is now as clear as the snow! The curse has passed away!'

Then, to our great sorrow, with a smile he died. He was a brave man, and we will never forget him.

Note by Jonathan Harker

Seven years have gone by. We are all happy now. Our boy was born a year from the day that Quincey Morris died. Mina hopes some of this man's bravery has passed into our child. We have named him Quincey.

We made a journey to Transylvania this summer. We visited the places which had filled us with so much terror. We can now hardly believe some of the things we saw with our own eyes and heard with our own ears. It all seems so far away. But the castle is still there. It is high upon a rock and it is still a frightening sight.

Arthur and Dr Seward are both happily married. The Professor often visits us and brings presents for the child.

Thank God for all his mercies and may the vampires never come back to the beautiful world in which we live!

The real history
of Dracula

The novel *Dracula* was written in 1897 by an Irish
actor–manager called Abraham (or 'Bram') Stoker.
He had wanted to write a vampire story for many
years, and spent months searching for ideas in the
British Museum. At last he found a German paper
describing the life of an evil Transylvanian prince
called Dracula, a man who was also known in history
as Vlad the Impaler.

Vlad was born in 1430. When he was fourteen years
old, his father had to leave him and his brother Radu
in the hands of the invading Turks, as hostages. Radu,
known as 'The Handsome', was a great favourite of
the Sultan. But Dracula terrified his guards by bribing
people to bring him small birds and animals, and then
torturing and impaling them on tiny sticks placed in
the ground.

This evil boy was released four years later. He then
began to fight against the Turks, and against anyone
else who stood in his way. Some of his crimes and
tortures are too terrible to write about. He was
believed to have killed 30000 people in one day. His
favourite method of execution was to impale victims
on stakes, and he would eat and drink amongst the
dreadful stench of dead bodies.

From this we see how Stoker got the idea of Renfield, of the idea of drinking human blood and of the horrible stink of Dracula's breath and burial places. It seems only fitting that the Impaler should be destroyed by a knife or stake through the heart.

Dracula was killed by the Turks when he was forty-five years old. His head was cut off and sent to the Sultan. His body was buried by his followers under the flagstones of the Monastery of Snagor, on an island near Bucharest in Roumania. When archaeologists opened up his grave they found only a shred of cloth, a ring and the bones of an ox.

Because of his victories over the Turks, Dracula is seen in his own country as a folk hero, rather like King Arthur, who will one day return to drive away all Roumania's enemies.

So we see that the history of Dracula is almost as strange, exciting and horrifying as the novel itself.

A GHOST HUNTER'S HANDBOOK

Peter Underwood

Long-time ghost expert and hunter, Peter Underwood, tells children all they need to know about ghosts, their habits and habitats. Peter Underwood, who is president of the Ghost Club and copyright holder of the only known photograph of a ghost, has written several books on ghosts for adults, but this is his first book on the subject for children. Serious in approach, it covers everything from how to find a ghost to information on ghosts that have been found in all parts of the world, and includes a section on famous ghosts and haunted houses that can be visited.

RICHARD BOLITHO – MIDSHIPMAN

Alexander Kent

It is October 1772 and the sixteen-year-old Richard Bolitho waits to join the *Gorgon*, a seventy-four-gun ship of the line.

Britain is at peace with her old enemies France and Spain; but pirates still threaten British trade routes and the slave trade between Africa and the Americas continues to flourish.

The *Gorgon* is ordered to sail to Africa's west coast to show the flag – and to destroy those who challenge the authority of the King's Navy. For Bolitho, and for many of the young, untrained crew, it is to be a testing time as they are pitted against a ruthless enemy.

THE PHANTOM SURFER

Carolyn Keene

Dana Girls Mystery No. 6: A series from the author of the Nancy Drew Books.

The town of Horizon had once been a thriving seaside resort, but had been allowed to run down until it was almost a ghost town.

It is here that the Dana girls, Jean and Louise, come with school friends for their spring holiday. Almost immediately, the Danas are plunged into the thick of a mystery. Not only do they witness a theft and discover that signals are being sent from an abandoned lighthouse, but they see for themselves the phantom-like surfer who appears only at night and vanishes before reaching the shore.

Amid all the fun of a surfing holiday, the teenage detectives must follow a twisting and treacherous trail before they solve this eerie mystery.

TIME BANDITS

Charles Alverson

Now a major film

Here one minute . . . there the next, from the Napoleonic Wars to Sherwood Forest, from Agamemnon's Greece to the deck of the doomed *Titanic*, a band of greedy dwarfs race through history. They are immortal yet human, timeless but always late, capable of inter-cosmic travel yet unable to tie their own shoelaces. Stealing in one century and hiding out in another, they are the most extraordinary gang ever let loose on this or any other universe.

They are the Time Bandits.

The Sparrow Bookshop

Sparrow has a whole nestful of exciting books that are available in bookshops or that you can order by post through the Sparrow Bookshop. Just complete the form below and enclose the money due and the books will be sent to you at home.

THE MYSTERY OF THE STONE TIGER	Carolyn Keene	95p	☐
THE PONY SEEKERS	D. Pullein-Thompson	95p	☐
THE NO-GOOD PONY	J. Pullein-Thompson	95p	☐
FLY-BY-NIGHT	K. M. Peyton	95p	☐
THE NEW TV SERIES OF WORZEL GUMMIDGE AND AUNT SALLY	Waterhouse and Hall	90p	☐
WORZEL GUMMIDGE AND THE TREASURE SHIP	B. E. Todd	95p	☐
RICHARD BOLITHO – MIDSHIPMAN	Alexander Kent	95p	☐
THE SPUDDY	Lillian Beckwith	85p	☐
AGAINST THE SEA	Douglas Reeman	95p	☐

Humour

LAUGH-A-MINUTE JOKE BOOK	Paul James	90p	☐
JELLYBONE GRAFITTI BOOK	Therese Birch	85p	☐
COMPLETE PRACTICAL JOKER	Peter Eldin	95p	☐
NEVER WEAR YOUR WELLIES IN THE HOUSE	Tom Baker	85p	☐

Total plus postage

And if you would like to hear more about our forthcoming books, write to the address below for the Sparrow News.

SPARROW BOOKS, BOOKSERVICE BY POST, PO BOX 29, DOUGLAS, ISLE OF MAN, BRITISH ISLES

Please enclose a cheque or postal order made out to Arrow Books Limited for the amount due including 8p per book for postage and packing for orders within the UK and 10p for overseas orders.

Please print clearly

NAME _____

ADDRESS _____

_____

Whilst every effort is made to keep prices down and popular books in print, Arrow Books cannot guarantee that prices will be the same as those advertised here or that the books will be available.